EIP-BW

ENTANGLED IN FREEDOM
A Civil War Story

Ann DeWitt & Kevin M. Weeks

Copyright © 2010 by Ann DeWitt & Kevin M. Weeks.

Library of Congress Control Number:		2010911635
ISBN:	Hardcover	978-1-4535-5526-2
	Softcover	978-1-4535-5525-5
	E-book	978-1-4535-5527-9

All rights reserved. No part of this book may be reproduced or transmitted in any form or by any means, electronic or mechanical, including photocopying, recording, or by any information storage and retrieval system without permission in writing from the copyright owners, except in the case of brief quotations embodied in critical articles and reviews. Purchase only authorized editions.

Company and product names mentioned herein are the trademarks or registered trademarks of their respective owners.

All scripture quotations in this book are from the *King James Version* of the Bible (KJV.)

This is a work of historical fiction. While the authors have used their best efforts in preparing this book, they make no representations or warranties with respect to the accuracy or completeness of the contents of this book. The voices that are presented in this book are derived from Ann DeWitt and Kevin M. Weeks' collaborative life experiences. Names, characters, places, businesses and incidents either are products of the authors' imagination or are used fictitiously and are not to be construed as real. Therefore, any similarity between names and stories of individuals described in this book and those individuals known to readers is inadvertent and purely coincidental.

This book was printed in the United States of America.

Visit our website *www.blackconfederatesoldiers.com* for additional information and resources for readers.

To order additional copies of this book, contact:
Xlibris Corporation
1-888-795-4274
www.Xlibris.com
Orders@Xlibris.com

This book is dedicated to all students, historians, educators, Civil War re-enactors and politicians who value the synthesis of information from different disciplines, the human capacity to reason, and the benefit of critical reflection.

Instrumental Historians

Gary Ray Goodson, Sr.
Georgia 40th Descendant
General Barton & Stovall History
~ Heritage Association, Historian Emeritus

Jonathan Green, National Park Ranger
Cumberland Gap National Historical Park
(Kentucky, Tennessee, Virginia)

Weldon Michael Griggs
General Barton & Stovall History
~ Heritage Association, President

Oxford Historical Shrine Society (Oxford, Georgia)

Edward Smith
Founder & Co-Director of the
American University Civil War Institute
Source: *Black Confederates*. DVD. Dixie Rising, 2008.

Nelson Winbush
Retired Assistant Principal and
Member of the Sons of Confederate Veterans (SCV)
Source: *A Man with a Message*. DVD. Dixie Depot, 2008.

Sites Visited

Atlanta History Center
(Atlanta, Georgia)

Mable House
(Mableton, Georgia)

Old Church and Kitty's Cottage
(Oxford, Georgia)

Olde Mill Inn Bed & Breakfast
(Cumberland Gap, Tennessee)

Southern Museum of Civil War and Locomotive History
(Kennesaw, Georgia)

Introduction

This fiction story is written for those who are open to equalize the historical landscape with facts about southern African-Americans who served during the American Civil War with the Confederate States Army. In this novel, *Entangled in Freedom*, the authors took creative liberty in providing their combined perspective on the American Civil War during the period when the 42nd Regiment Georgia Volunteers C.S.A. enlisted and later fought at Cumberland Gap, Tennessee.

In addition, this book is a spin-off of the Green family in the crime fiction novel titled *The Street Life Series: Is It Rags or Riches?* by Kevin M. Weeks. Every effort was made to neither rewrite American history nor speak for all African-Americans on this subject matter. Most historical accounts occurred during the period of March 1862 to October 1862. Also, the slave language is translated into 21st century vernacular for clarity of dialogue while staying true, as possible, to the 19th century era. Sources, in which this imaginative exposition was derived, are also included.

Let us not disregard the heritage of any African-American freedman or slave who ultimately made tough life or death choices on the freedom road in which he or she labored in paving the way for many generations to travel on this day.

Ann DeWitt &
Kevin M. Weeks

The Green Farm

(March 1862)

1. The Green Farmhouse
2. kitchen house
3. Isaac's shotgun house
4. Momma Annabel's shotgun house
5. stables
6. & 7. Isaac brothers' shotgun houses
8. pea fields
9. courtyard
10. outhouse

Chapter 1

HORSE HOOVES POUNDED the red Georgia dirt as dust filled the air. No visitors were expected at the Green Farm on this gloomy 5th instant of March 1862. Since America was in the midst of a Civil War, I ran out of the smokehouse with Master Green's sharp edged axe because I thought the farm was under attack. As I prepared to throw the axe at the trespasser, the dust settled before I could make out the face. I yelled, "Stop or I'll kill you!"

"Isaac, is that you? Put that thing away," demanded a familiar southern English voice.

"Yes sir, it's me, Mr. Fair."

"My, oh my, you get taller and taller every time I see you. What are you? . . . about six feet now? Rosa Lee better watch out for those other slave girls who might take a liking to you." As he laughed, his belly jiggled.

I asked, "What's the matter? Is Mrs. Fair alright? Do you need me to go get Momma Annabel to deliver the baby?"

"No, but hurry, hurry, go into the house and tell Abraham that I need to speak with him immediately!" he exclaimed as he stepped down from the horse-drawn carriage. On this Wednesday, Mr. Marty Fair wore a pair of black trousers and a plain white cotton shirt. As sweat beaded down his buff beige face, I noticed that his grey hair was thinning and his deep blue eyes suddenly turned more cold than usual.

I placed the axe in the corner of the smokehouse and walked quickly into the backdoor of the two-story Georgian farmhouse. A central hallway and two rooms on both sides were on each level. Unexpectedly, Master Abraham Green was already up and stirring. Then I heard my wife, Rosa Lee, who was bringing in the hot breakfast on a silver tray from the outside kitchen house.

Inside of the main house, Master Green asked, "Who goes there?"

I said, "It's Mr. Fair. He says that he needs to tell you something; and it's urgent."

"Well, bring him to the sitting room," Master Green said in an hospitable southern tone. Then he turned to Rosa Lee and said, "Add another setting to the table so that Marty can have breakfast with me."

"Yes sir," she said almost bumping into me and nearly spilling the crisp pieces of bacon, boiled eggs and a bowl of grits onto the floor.

As I escorted Mr. Fair into the house, he practically knocked me over going from room to room searching for Master Green before I could say a word.

"Abraham! Abraham! Where are you?"

I said, "He's in the sitting room, Mr. Fair."

"Isaac, why didn't you tell me that to begin with?"

The sitting room was painted a bright yellow. An upholstered blue and yellow striped sofa with matching Gainsborough chairs were in a U-configuration. Entering into the room, Mr. Fair said to Master Green, "What's this talk I hear of you going to war?"

"Is that what has you stirring so early before the break of dawn—the war?" asked Master Green.

"Yes, I just got wind that you are going off to Camp McDonald on tomorrow. Tell me that you are not volunteering. This is insane. How old are you now? . . . 63?"

Master Green was a stately man with brown eyes and classic ivory skin. Standing about six feet tall, he was very healthy from walking around the 126 acre farm. He said, "Actually, I'm 54. Do I look that old to you?"

"You are no longer a young man is my point," said Mr. Fair.

Entering into the room, Rosa Lee said, "Breakfast is on the table."

Remembering to remove his hat, Mr. Fair said, "Why hello there Ms. Rosa Lee, you look mighty pretty today."

Rosa Lee's natural cocoa skin beamed as she exited the room in her exquisite pink petticoat dress with a white Pinner Apron tied around her hourglass waist. I felt a sense of jealously at Mr. Fair's compliment; however, I agreed with him.

"My wife, Sally, keeps making all of these dresses and putting them on Rosa Lee. You'd think Sally was a professional dressmaker. She tells me that when her lady friends come for tea and see the dresses on Rosa Lee that someone buys a dress," said Master Green leading the way into the adjoining grey dining room.

Breakfast and dinner meals were very formal in the Green house. The best china was always used because Master Green said that you can't take any material things with you when you die. White Porcelain china trimmed in gold with a crystal glass full of orange juice was on the lace white tablecloth. Not one piece of the silver flatware was out of place at the rectangular maple dining table with six chairs.

As he sat down, Master Green said, "Well, I was talking to Robert Mable, my distant cousin by marriage who lives in Mill Grove, Georgia. He said that the Union Soldiers will not likely harm the women and slaves if we men go off to war. Besides, I have plenty of fresh water in the well and meat in the smokehouse. Robert believes that if Sally and our slaves are kind to the soldiers that perhaps my property will not be harmed."

"Here you go again giving up before the war has barely started. The Confederacy is going to win this war, if not in battle, then in the hearts and minds of the people."

Turning his head towards me, Master Green said, "I'm taking Isaac with me. He is the best horse rider in the state of Georgia. Believe me, I plan to come back home alive."

Mr. Fair said, "Isaac, do you mind if I speak with Abraham alone?"

"No sir. Master Green, is there anything else I can help you with this morning?"

"No, you go and get the horses ready for the long trip," said Master Green.

I walked out of the backdoor of the main house and looked out across the Green Farm. We slaves lived a few yards away in the backyard. There were a total of four slave houses, each with a single door in the front and the back. We called them shotgun houses because if someone shot through the front door, the bullet would travel directly through the backdoor. Each house was one room wide and two rooms deep.

There were two houses per row. The two houses on the front faced the back of the main house with my house on the left and my mother's on the right. The two houses on the back row faced the southern pea fields and were occupied by my slave brothers. There were eight of us in all.

The center tract of Georgia red clay where the back of the slaves' houses met was a makeshift courtyard. This created a quick passageway between our homes. As an example, I could leave out of the back of my house and go straight into the backdoor of my brothers' house. The same held true for the other two houses. This arrangement created a sense of slave community away from the main house.

We slaves on the front row were the house slaves; and my brothers on the back row tended the fields. Master Green did not hold in any greater esteem his house slaves from his field slaves. In fact, sometimes I wish I were assigned to the southern pea field because the field slaves were out in the open air. Regardless, slave labor was not easy.

On this morning, the prayers of my momma, Annabel, sounded throughout the slave quarters. She prayed, "Dear Lord, please bless us on this day. May the fruits of our labor be for the good in the building of your kingdom . . ." Who needs a rooster to crow when you have a mother who prays out loud at 5am in the morning? Master Green thought Momma Annabel was praying for the crops to have a profitable harvest. She was really praying that Master Green wouldn't sell her to another slaveholder. Since Momma Annabel lived through about 48 cold winters, she knew that she would not be able to conceive any more children soon, and slave children grew up to be the workers in the fields. Ultimately, the fields brought about wealth for the Green family.

The lightning flashed through the window of our small slave quarters as I opened the door and looked into Rosa Lee's eyes. Over one year ago, Master Green, who was also a travelling minister, arranged and performed my marriage to Rosa Lee. After the wedding, he said that even if the marriage was not legal in the state of Georgia, that our marriage was ordained by God.

I knew that the decision I was about to make would change the course of our family lineage, perhaps forever. Rosa Lee's smile was soft, and she exhibited a display of confidence in me that I did not have within myself. After I placed our nine month old baby boy, Jacob, in the hand-woven oval brown wicker cradle, the warmth of Rosa Lee's body as we embraced consumed every innate desire I had for her since we courted as teenagers from adjoining southern farms.

"Isaac, I don't want you to go worrying about us. Through prayer, I know God has already delivered us to a better life," said Rosa Lee.

"I know you are right. I'm just trying to reconcile in my own mind what others will think of me if I choose to bear arms and fight," I said.

Straightening up my crisp linen grey shirt collar, she sighed and said, "You have never worried about what folk have said about you in the past. I don't see why you have to start now. You turn a deaf ear to the slaves from the other plantations who call you a Jeff Davis man; yet you deal with Master Green treating you like a child every single day."

"You know that I get along with everybody. I have learned to set aside those things. This is not about me. When they tell you that your husband is fighting to stay a slave, what will you say? When they tell you that I'm a prisoner of war in this very country, captured by the Union, how will you feel?"

She tilted her head slightly and said, "I am a Dunbar woman. Women in my family have seen harder times than this for me to worry about what folks say. When I saw families separated at the Savannah port, I held my head up and told myself that I was going to get through this. When I was chosen to work in the home of a southern farmhouse, I knew that God had answered my prayer."

Hastily I said, "See, this is exactly what I'm talking about. People don't confront you today when you say things like this because I'm around to protect you. You can't go talking like that when I'm gone to war or people will isolate you even further from civilization." I placed a hand on each of Rosa Lee's shoulders and extended my arms to see her facial expression better.

She looked intensely into my dark brown eyes and said, "Mrs. Green is going to make sure that I'm busy sewing up the Confederate soldier uniforms with the others while you are gone. I'll be fine; I say."

As I embraced her once again, I took a deep breath and said, "You are right. I know you will. Master Green says that the Confederate soldiers are dropping like flies and they need more arms and legs. What will you tell our baby boy Jacob if I die?"

"You are going to live. Stop talking like that." She turned her back away from me to suppress the tears. "When you get back, we will tell our son that you decided to put your family first like any man would do given the same opportunity. You weighed your options; and it's better for us to stay in the south where we know there is food, clothes and shelter, than to go trusting a government that turned its head as we disembarked from slave ships."

I reached over to the brown oak table and picked up the white sheet of paper with Master Green's written agreement to free me if I fought in the Civil War. I chuckled and said, "I don't know how you muster up the courage to face a potential mob of people from both sides."

Instead of replying, Rosa Lee placed her head gently on my shoulder.

For some reason, Master Green strongly advised that I serve side by side with him in the Confederacy as part of the 42nd Regiment Georgia Volunteers. Some of the white indentured servants thought that black slave men like me would turn the guns on them if we fought together in the Civil War; and the black men who stayed behind called me a traitor of the emancipation cause for all. Regardless of what either side thought, both the white indentured servants and we African slaves both longed for a life like Master Green.

However, on this day, my resolve to serve the Confederacy in whatever capacity needed was centered on keeping my family safe and insuring that my seed for generations to come were free forever. Thinking in the present was all I could do because my family's future was never clear. I was torn between two factions. What did it matter anyway? My opinion on the matter was already ignored for the greater good. This is my story.

Chapter 2

I HEARD MRS. Sally Green yelling, "Isaac, Isaac . . . Isaac!"

Without hesitation, I dashed through the backdoor of the main house, and the screen door slammed behind me. "What is it, Mrs. Sally?"

With bright blue eyes and blonde hair pulled back into a bun, Mrs. Sally was one of the most beautiful women in Oxford. Her natural ivory skin glistened from her morning beauty routine. This morning, she wore a simple navy blue long length dress. Running towards the backdoor, she grabbed my hand and pleaded like a true Southern Belle, "You have to go into the sitting room and talk to Abraham. After Marty left, Abraham will not say a word to me. He has been in there for hours. Isaac, I know he will talk to you."

I never understood why Mrs. Sally always depended on me. Maybe it is because Master Green and she did not have any children. Momma Annabel told me that Mrs. Sally gave birth to one still born baby boy and was never pregnant again.

Hurriedly, Mrs. Sally led the way down the narrow hall back to the sitting room. Staring out of the window, Master Green was seated in the blue and yellow striped Gainsborough chair. I said, "Mrs. Sally asked me to see if you needed anything."

There was no response. I wondered if he had died sitting in that chair. I walked over to touch him on the shoulder and asked, "Master Green?"

Still, there was no response. I almost cursed because if he died all of my chances of owning the farm in middle Georgia were out the window.

He startled me when he said, "Isaac, I swear on my father's grave in Dublin, Georgia that I cannot take any more of these conflicts in the south." His face was cherry red as if he were ready to slug someone.

"What's wrong?"

"Sit down and let me tell you a story." I sat down on the sofa across from him, and he continued, "Marty just told me that if I go to war and take you with me that I might ruin my chances of ever becoming a bishop in the United Methodist Church. I've been studying theology for years."

"Yes sir, I know you have; and we enjoy hearing your sermons when you are invited to speak."

Turning to look me in the eyes, he continued, "When you were four years old, Bishop James O. Andrew inherited a slave named Kitty . . ."

"I've heard the slaves around the way speak of Kitty. What do you know about the reverend?"

"Bishop Andrew was the chairman of Emory College and a bishop of the United Methodist Church right here in Oxford." When he looked up, Mrs. Sally passed Master Green a cold glass of lemonade and left the room. There was a sigh of relief on her face. He added, "Well, the United Methodist Church stated that Bishop Andrew couldn't own a slave even if he inherited one, but Georgia State law wouldn't allow the bishop to free Kitty either."

"Do say?"

"Bishop Andrew was caught between a rock and a hard place. That single incident split the northern and southern branches of the United Methodist Church. That's why they call our church Methodist Episcopal Church South."

"I don't rightly understand what this has to do with your going to war."

He shifted his weight from his right leg to his left leg and said, "Marty didn't come out and say it, but I think he believes the church folk up north will think I'm fighting to keep you and your family slaves. Perhaps this means that I can only be ordained as a bishop in the south."

Mrs. Sally must have been listening at the door. Because for the first time in my life, she passed me a cold glass of lemonade; and by Momma Annabel's account, I lived about 22 cold winters.

When Mrs. Sally left the sitting room, I asked, "Did you tell Mr. Fair that I have a document from you stating that I will be free; and I can have your father's property in Dublin, Georgia if I bring you back from the war alive?"

Turning cherry red again, Master Green said, "That is none of his business what agreement I have with you."

I knew to keep quiet because Master Green's temper could flare up at any given moment.

He continued, "Now I have to make a choice. I can stay here. If I stay, the Confederates may think that I don't support the cause, and they might burn the house down. On the other hand, if I stay, the Union soldiers may think that I'm imprisoning you and the others, and the Union might incinerate everything to set you all free. Or I can go to war to better the chances of all being saved." He looked at me to see if I was following his logic. Then he added, "Marty is causing me to rethink everything."

I allowed a minute or two of silence to hang in the air before I said, "The way I see it; family comes first. I can no longer think about what people will say. The Union is not offering me a chance of owning any house or land."

Right then and there, I thought Master Green was going to cry because he knew that everything in the universe was aligning to change.

I asked, "Whatever happened to Kitty?"

"The last will and testament of Bishop Andrew's first wife stated that when Kitty came of age, she could choose to move to Liberia or stay in America."

"Where is Liberia?"

"Liberia is in Africa. The American Colonization Society made arrangements over twenty years ago for slaves who were freed by their masters to move to Liberia."

"What did Kitty do?"

"She decided to stay on Bishop Andrew's property in a broken down shed that the bishop converted into, what Sally calls, a quaint saddlebag house."

"Really?"

"Yes, I heard that Kitty was terrified to take another trip back to Africa on a ship that might take a six month journey. She remembered firsthand that half the black people died on the slave ships coming to America. Plus, she didn't want to smell the feces and be in deplorable conditions again. The memories she had from the slave ship were horrific."

"Momma Annabel and Rosa Lee shared their stories about coming over on slave ships in chains and all. I'm glad I was born here because I don't think I could go through what Momma Annabel and Rosa Lee went through."

There was silence because Master Green didn't know how to respond. By choice, he was totally unaware of the gut-wrenching details of Momma Annabel and Rosa Lee's travels to America.

So I continued and said, "Momma Annabel came across the waters tens of summers ago from Egypt by way of the Arab-Muslim Slave Trade. However, Rosa Lee only remembers coming over to America a few summers ago as a young girl through the Port of Philadelphia on a ship called the New Hanover. Later, Rosa Lee was transported to Savannah, Georgia. Rosa Lee thinks she has seen at least 27 winters now. Like Kitty, they both say that they are not going back to Africa."

Still, there was only silence. Taking a chance to put things out in the open, I added, "The story you tell about Kitty is not the story the slaves around here are saying about Kitty and the reverend."

Taking a sip of lemonade and crossing his legs, he asked, "What are they saying?"

"I don't mean to be disrespectful about the reverend. However, they say that after the reverend's wife died, the reverend and Kitty fell in love. The reverend couldn't live without Kitty."

Standing up quickly, Master Green exclaimed, "That's hearsay; Bishop Andrew is an honorable man!"

"I'm sorry I upset you. I should just be quiet," I said turning my head towards the window.

"No, I want to hear what they are saying," he said with a fist closed on each of his hips.

"Well, they say that Kitty has children by the reverend."

"That's enough! You are right, you should be quiet," he said pacing the floor. "What else are they saying?"

"On the other hand, Momma Annabel says that Kitty never existed. She has never seen her; and Oxford is a small place."

"Hogwash, Annabel is afraid to step one foot off of this farm, and that's why she has never seen Kitty. Besides, I don't travel in the same social circles as the bishop."

"I will say this."

". . . and what is that?" he asked with a cherry red face as he sat back down.

"I agree with Kitty. I wouldn't want to take that long journey back on a ship to Africa either. I wouldn't know how to find my family there."

When I said this, Master Green leaned forward in the chair.

ENTANGLED IN FREEDOM: A CIVIL WAR STORY | 13

I added, "I don't want to go up north either. We are in the middle of a war. Where would I go? A few months ago, the Union soldiers brought some slaves back to their slave masters in Covington. The soldiers said that their Union camps were too crowded to keep runaway slaves."

Somehow I managed to get Master Green to smile. I asked, "Can you explain to me why this country would give a slave a choice to go back to Africa?"

He turned to look out the window again and said, "Isaac, it's extremely complicated. There are so many things that I want to tell you. As we travel together throughout the war, I am going to share a great deal of things with you."

"I'd like that Master Green."

He turned to me and said, "Do you know why I trust you and no one else?"

"No," I said finishing off the lemonade.

"My boy, you have earned my trust over the years. I can tell you the deepest darkest secrets and it goes nowhere." Then he slapped his thighs with his hands and stood up.

As if they were joined together at the hip, Mrs. Sally came to the door; and Master Green walked over to Mrs. Sally and gave her a big hug and kiss. Then she said, "Isaac, I told you that you were the only person who can get Abraham to talk when he gets in his bad moods. How about this? Since this is the night before you go off to war with Abraham, I want you to take the baby over to Annabel's, and I will give Rosa Lee the evening off around 6:30."

"I'd like that," I said standing up.

Momma Annabel once told me that after we slaves were locked in our quarters for the evening that Mrs. Sally would come get baby Jacob and take him back to the main house. I always thought Mrs. Sally was genuine about her feelings for baby Jacob, but Momma Annabel said that Mrs. Sally wanted to bond with baby Jacob. In this way, Jacob wouldn't grow up to become a runaway slave. Momma Annabel said that children who feel nurtured by the slave master are less likely to runaway. I'm also told that Mrs. Sally once cared for me in the same manner when I was a baby.

Interrupting my thoughts, Master Green said, "Isaac, I need you to go across town before dark and tell Marty that I am going to fight at Cumberland Gap. I'll deal with things when I get back." He rubbed his stomach and said, "I missed lunch. Let me get ready for supper."

Picking up the two empty glasses, I saw that Master Green had been writing into a book of some sort. After I left the main house, I went into the kitchen house which was a separate building. The kitchen was not attached to the main house as a fire precaution; because if the kitchen house caught on fire, the main house might be saved from destruction.

From the side window, I could see the other slaves working in the southern pea fields. I became home sick already and wondered if I would see my family again.

Without notice, Rosa Lee walked up from behind me and gave me a big hug. Then I turned around to give her a kiss, and she said, "It's too bad that we can't spend time together before you go to that Gap place."

"The Gap place is called Cumberland Gap. It's the point where Tennessee, Virginia, and Kentucky all meet. If we don't stop the Union Army, they will be headed straight for Oxford. The Union calls Cumberland Gap the gateway into the Deep South." When she didn't say a word, teasingly I said, "I have some good news for you."

"Pray tell, what could it be?" she asked nestled up against my neck.

"Mrs. Sally is giving you the night off."

Lifting her head, she asked, "Why? She and Master Green want us to make another baby to work in the field? I don't want to be a baby making machine like my mother."

"Shhh!" I said putting my hand gently across her mouth, ". . . before they hear you."

Moving my hand, she said, "Well, you know it's true."

"This time, Mrs. Sally just wants us to spend private time together. So why don't you think of what we are going to do tonight while I go over to Mr. Fair's farmhouse."

Because we slaves were locked into our houses at night, I knew that if Rosa Lee didn't prepare early, the night would be the same old boring routine. Then I heard footsteps, as if Mrs. Sally were reading my mind. She walked into the kitchen house and said, "Rosa Lee, what are you and Isaac going to do tonight?"

"There ain't nothing for us to do, Mrs. Sally, but sleep."

With a great big smile, she said, "Why don't you come upstairs and let me see what I can conjure up for the two of you?"

"Mrs. Sally, are you feeling well? Why you being so nice to me and—"

"Mrs. Sally, what Rosa Lee is trying to say is thank you for allowing us to have some time by ourselves tonight. Whatever you do, we certainly appreciate," I said as I nudged Rosa Lee.

Knowing that I needed to be back before dark, I headed over to the right side of the farm where the horse stables were located. I decided that I was going to ride the black American Saddlebred named Midnight to Mr. Fair's farmhouse. After I pushed my feet off of the ground, I gently lowered onto the saddle. Out of nowhere there was a big BOOM!

Chapter 3

IMMEDIATELY, MIDNIGHT STOPPED and reared up on its hind legs. Thinking quickly, I grabbed the horse by the neck and slid off until my feet touched the ground; otherwise, Midnight could have trampled me to death. Where was the source of the sound? Upon the heavens was a dark sky, and the winds were moving the clouds to a distant place. I knew that if I didn't deliver the message to Mr. Fair soon, I would be caught in the upcoming thunderstorm.

Thinking that Midnight would not ride well in the storm, I took him back to the stable. Then I saddled the bay American Saddlebred named Daybreak. BOOM! As the thunder sounded, Daybreak began to gallop at a steady speed.

Within the hour, I was in front of Mr. Fair's white picket fence. Then I heard men screaming like cowboys. When I dismounted the horse, a man came up to me quickly and handcuffed my hands behind my back. I said, "Redhead Wilson, what are you doing? I ain't done nothing wrong."

Before Wilson, who was an indentured servant of Mr. Fair, shoved me in the back of a wagon, I glimpsed into the eyes of one of Mr. Fair's slave boys named Raymond. I knew when Raymond started to run that he would send for help. Because slave children were not permitted to leave their slave master's farm, each child would run as fast as he or she could through the woods and fields to the property line. Then that child would give the South African war cry to the neighboring child and convey the verbal report. This continued until the last child reached the final destination for the message to be delivered. At the end of this marathon, my younger brother knocked on the backdoor of Momma Annabel's slave house.

"Momma Annabel, they got Isaac. Redhead Wilson picked him up and pushed him hard in the back of a wagon," said my slave brother Jeremiah who lived for at least 11 cold winters.

Wearing a white prairie dress, Momma Annabel ran into the main house screaming, "Master Green! Master Green! . . . Master Green!"

"What in the world are you all upset about Annabel?" he asked.

"Redhead Wilson done got Isaac. They took him into Covington, but I don't know where."

Without any more questions, Master Green ran out to the horse stable, saddled the white American Saddlebred named Sunlight, and the horse galloped away. By this time, the rain poured down, and the Georgia dust began to transform into Georgia red clay.

In Covington, I heard Master Green walk into the one room jailhouse where I was being held in handcuffs and chains. While I sat on an eight foot long pine wood Deacon's Bench, Wilson paced the wooden floor back and forth. There were no other prisoners in the three cells. However, I knew this place would be packed by the time the weekend rolled around because of the Friday night brawling and gambling.

Taking off his Mackintosh raincoat, Master Green said to Wilson, "I want to speak with Marty."

Within a few minutes, Mr. Fair, who was also the Sheriff, came into the building while closing his rain napper. "Why hello there Abraham, what can I do you for?" asked Mr. Fair pulling back the wooden chair from his mahogany partner's desk.

"Let Isaac go this minute."

"Well, the law states that black folk can't be out on the streets past dusk."

"Marty, the sun hasn't even set yet."

Taking a seat at the desk and rummaging through the center drawer, Mr. Fair said, "By the way, Isaac can't travel unless he has papers." Yelling to me across the room, Mr. Fair said, "Do you have any papers on you that say you reside in Oxford? I can't find anything in my desk!"

Before I could answer, Master Green asked, "What papers are required to travel from town to town? Isaac has been coming to your farmhouse since he could ride a pony. What is this nonsense?"

"Well, if black folk are going to be emancipated, we need to know who they are and where they are from."

"Marty, you know Isaac," Master Green said pointing his finger.

"Well, these aren't the only charges I have on him. He pulled out an axe on me this morning. That is possession of a deadly weapon and attempted murder."

Master Green turned cherry red and asked, "Did he pull out the axe on my property?"

"Well, as a matter of fact he did."

"Then you were trespassing, and Isaac has a right to protect my property, especially during this American Civil War!" he exclaimed pushing Wilson to the side so that he could pace the floor.

Mr. Fair said, "That leads me to another infraction. You haven't paid the tax increase for your eight slaves. The state is anticipating that if the Union wins this war, taxes are going to go up significantly. The north has come up with a very elaborate tax system, and we are preparing for the worst in Georgia. If you don't pay the balance of what you owe by morning, your slaves will become the property of the state of Georgia. The bidding for Isaac starts at dawn."

My heart raced and beads of sweat rolled down my brow. Over the years, mere conversations were the closest I came to witnessing the cruelty to slaves. At the Green Farm, the slave driver was responsible for punishing the misbehaved slaves. Not until now did I realize that the enormous world outside of my small domain was vastly different.

"Have you lost your mind? I haven't even received a tax notice," said Master Green stopping in his tracks.

"No, Abraham. YOU have lost YOUR mind. We can't allow you to take Isaac to Cumberland Gap. Nobody will come and do business in these parts if you go off to war with a slave."

"What about Wilson?"

"What about him?"

"He is just as much a slave as Isaac. Is President Lincoln freeing Wilson too? Wilson stood in the town square to be sold to the highest bidder just as Rosa Lee in days gone by. So are you saying that no involuntary indentured servant should go off to war?"

Mr. Fair looked stumped. I don't think he thought of Wilson as a slave because Wilson was Irish with pale bisque skin. Indentured servants were pretty much enslaved as the African slave; however, indentured servants possessed greater rights and were released within a few years after their servitude.

Mr. Fair said, "That's preposterous."

Turning to Wilson, Master Green said, "Wilson, why don't you head on over to Atlanta and find you and your family a new home."

Wilson said, "Mr. Green, you know I can't do that. I can't leave until the date on my papers has expired."

Mr. Fair said, "That proves nothing."

Putting his left foot on the Deacon's bench, Master Green said, "Okay Wilson, lift up your shirt and show us your back."

Lifting up his shirt, Wilson's face turned red, and I gasped. There were whip marks all over Wilson's back.

"Stop it! Stop it!" yelled Mr. Fair, "You are trying to humiliate Wilson in front of Isaac."

Master Green said, "Well, tell me how Wilson got all of those scars on his back?"

"Okay, two can play this game," said Mr. Fair who pushed Master Green's foot off the bench. "Isaac, turn around."

I turned around slowly not knowing what Mr. Fair was going to do. I braced myself to get my whipping. After lifting up the back of my shirt, Mr Fair said, "Oh my." Then Mr. Fair took off the handcuffs and the chains from my feet. He demanded, "Isaac, take off all of your clothes, now!" Naked and ashamed, I turned around slowly before him, Wilson, and Master Green. Mr. Fair said, "Oh my."

There was not one mark or bruise on my pecan tanned skin. Sure, I had been beaten by the slave driver over the years. Master Green established rules about how slaves were to be beaten because he regarded slaves as his prize property. He would always say that prize property was worth more than gold. Then after all beatings, Momma Annabel would tenderly rub me down with cocoa butter as she scolded me for being disobedient.

Hastily, Mr. Fair said, "Isaac, put back on your clothes now." Then he paced the floor back and forth.

Laughing, Master Green said, "You don't look good, Marty."

Pounding his fist in his hand, Mr. Fair came face to face with Master Green and said, "You listen to me and you hear me good, Abraham. I can hang you and Isaac right here and now." Turning to Wilson, Mr. Fair said, "Put those cuffs and chains back on Isaac."

As the sound of the metal chains clashed against the wooden floor, the cornerstone of Covington walked into the jailhouse shaking the rain off of her black folding parasol. Mrs. Jessica Fair, an elderly woman who lived to see 80 cold winters, pointed her finger and said, "Marty, what do I hear about you snatching Isaac up this evening?" Her porcelain ivory skin was radiant as ever. Standing less than five feet tall, Mr. Fair's mother continued, "Isaac isn't one of the rebellious ones. You are going to turn Isaac against us, and we need him. Other slaves look up to Isaac and want to be like him."

Out of respect, Mr. Fair, who lived to see about 60 winters, was too embarrassed to speak. In the south, there was an unwritten code of conduct that elders were to be respected regardless of the surrounding circumstances.

With her right hand, she lifted the bottom of her blue hoopskirt with a promenade bodice top, walked over to Wilson and asked, "How long have you and Isaac been playing together in the fields?"

Wilson said, "But Mr. Fair told me to take Isaac. I had no other choice but to do it or I would get a whipping myself."

I believed that God was working in the midst of the conflict. Mrs. Fair was a spit fire in getting her way. Within about nine minutes or so, I was standing behind Master Green with the cuffs and chains removed.

"Mrs. Fair, thank you so much for helping me square things away on Issac," said Master Green.

"I am not finished with you either, Abraham. Do I hear correctly that you are going off to war with the 42nd Regiment Georgia Volunteers?"

"Yes ma'am."

"Do you not know that I have a son who is enlisted in the United States 1st Tennessee Infantry fighting for the Union?"

"I didn't know that," said Master Green.

"Did you know that the 42nd Regiment Georgia Volunteers will be assigned to the Confederate Forces Department of East Tennessee? Are you getting the picture, son?" she asked as she combed her shiny silver grey hair with her right fingers.

The room was quiet. I didn't understand the question and wondered if either Mr. Fair or Master Green understood what she was asking.

She continued, "Let me break it down for you boys. When you go to Cumberland Gap, southern grandsires, fathers, uncles, bubs, and cousins will be fighting against each other."

Breaking the silence, Master Green said, "Marty, you fed me some cockamamie story about Bishop Andrew being dismissed from the United Methodist Church for owning Kitty. Was she his only slave?"

Mrs. Fair leaned forward and said, "It's neither here nor there if Bishop James O. Andrew owned one slave or twelve. He wasn't suppose to own any based on the United Methodist Church."

Turning to Mr. Fair, Master Green added, "Why didn't you tell me that your brother from Tennessee would be fighting for the Union at Cumberland Gap? All this time, we could have been talking about the real issue."

Mr. Fair said, "I was embarrassed."

"Embarrassed?" asked Master Green.

"My brother is a traitor of the south. I wasn't going to tell you that he was fighting for the north. What would you think of my English family?"

Mrs. Fair said, "I love all of my sons the same. Abraham, you go on and fight at Cumberland Gap. Personally, I think you are wasting your time. I can't see southern relatives fighting against each other south of the 36-degrees-30-minutes latitude line." She wiped the perspiration from her forehead and added, "It's a shrewd move of the north to wager a skirmish between southern brothers, all for a critical track of mountain land that leads into the Deep South." I could tell that she was tired of standing because of the way she was leaning on her left foot. She continued, "Marty, Abraham, have a seat at the table over there with me. Wilson, you go over there with Isaac and sit down."

As Wilson and I watched them converse around the square walnut table, I tried my best to understand what just happened. I asked Wilson, "Did Master Green just call you a slave?"

With pride, the young man, whom I played with at the Green Farm for at least 18 summers, said, "I am not a slave, but an indentured servant. There's a big difference. When I have children, they will be free. Your son Jacob is born a slave. Plus, in a few years, my service to Mr. Fair will end. Isaac, you will remain a slave forever. Perhaps, I will buy Jacob one day."

My hands tightened into fists; however, I dared not show my true emotions. For some unknown reason, Wilson's arrogance compelled me to want to fight in this Civil War. I was going to bring Master Green back alive if it was the last thing I did. My family was destined to live free at the farm in Dublin, Georgia. After all, Mrs. Fair said that it would be unlikely for brother to fight against brother at Cumberland Gap. As I saw things, my odds were even better than I originally thought.

Mrs. Fair said, "Wilson, go get us something to drink."

This angered Wilson, because Mrs. Fair didn't ask me to go retrieve the drink. To be frank, I don't understand myself why she chose Wilson over me. Perhaps, she was still mad at him for cuffing me. By the way, when Mrs. Fair said "us," she was not including Wilson and me in having any tea.

When Wilson did not move, she said, "Go on. We are waiting Wilson."

Chapter 4

AFTER WILSON RETURNED with the sweetened tea, Mrs. Fair turned to me and said, "Isaac, come on over here and sit down. You need to hear this too."

I turned around to see if there was another Isaac in the room.

She said, "Don't take all day, son."

Reluctantly, I pulled the chair from under the table and sat down against the wall because this was all new to me.

"I didn't say sit over there, Isaac. I said sit at the table with us."

Beads of sweat started to roll down my face again, and I said, "Yes, ma'am."

"Abraham, you and Isaac need to know a few things before you go off to Cumberland Gap. We neighbors in Newton County stick together. There is a rumor that R. J. Henderson is going to be one of the colonels in the 42nd. R. J. is from outside of Covington. I've gotten word to him to look out for you and Isaac. He sent me a message back stating that he would," she said taking a sip of tea.

Master Green said, "That's mighty nice of you. However, I don't understand why it matters."

"I'll tell you why. In the state of Georgia only 10% of us are slaveholders; whereas in Tennessee there are about 25% slaveholders. That means that the majority of the men fighting at Cumberland Gap do not own slaves. Abraham, I believe that they will think you are a planter."

"But I'm a yeoman farmer, I'm not rich," Master Green said turning to Mr. Fair.

She said, "When you show up with Isaac, many people will assume you own hundreds of slaves, not just the eight."

Master Green said, "Let me be very clear. Sally inherited Annabel from her parents. I have never bought a slave in my life."

Mr. Fair said, "That's my point about Bishop Andrew. He inherited Kitty too, and you see where that got him—dismissed from the United Methodist Church."

Standing up, Master Green exclaimed, "Stop it! You know this has nothing to do with Bishop Andrew and everything to do with your brother fighting for the Union!"

"Sit down, Abraham," Mrs. Fair said calmly while wiping the sweat from her brow.

"Where was I? Oh yes, about 75% of the men fighting at Cumberland Gap will care less about slavery because they don't own any slaves. You must understand this before you set foot at Camp McDonald in Big Shanty. Be prepared."

"Prepared for what?" asked Master Green tapping his fingers on the table.

"Have your answer ready as to why you are taking a slave with you to fight in this war," she said.

"I don't owe anybody an explanation. I've already done my research. Lieutenant Colonel Marcellus Stovall with the 3rd Georgia Infantry Battalion is already travelling with his colored bodyguard named Josiah. It's quite possible that Issac and I will be attached to the same brigade. Do you get the picture?" he asked sarcastically.

"Marcellus Stovall from Augusta, Georgia?" she asked.

"Yes, ma'am," said Master Green with a smirk thinking that he finally got one over on Mrs. Fair.

"I thought Marcellus had rheumatism," she said with a chuckle.

"Well, he is enlisted with the Confederate States Army now," said Master Green.

"What's rheumatism?" I asked hesitantly because I didn't know if I was really invited to join in the conversation.

She said, "Rheumatism is a pain some people get in the joints of their body. How is Marcellus Stovall going to get up the mountains around Cumberland Gap with rheumatism?" When no one answered, she added, "What do you know about Tennessee, Abraham?"

Master Green stood up as if he were going to walk out the door and said, "What's with all of the questions, Mrs. Fair? I don't see why it matters. As I see it, no one can really prepare for this war."

"Abraham, I said sit down."

Glimpsing at me, Master Green must have remembered that he owed her for releasing me. So, he sat back down and took a swig of the tea.

She added, "I asked you a question. What do you know about Tennessee?"

"I know that this will be mountain warfare which requires the fitness of young men, and that's why I'm taking Isaac."

She said, "That's not the important thing to know. Tennessee is in the middle of a feud. Western and Southern Tennessee are for the Confederates, and Eastern Tennessee is for the Union. In some Eastern Tennessee villages, the people are split right down the middle between the Confederates and the Union. My guess is that Cumberland Gap is going to be swarming with Union soldiers who were born and raised in the south. I'm just trying to prepare you, son."

"Do say?" I said before Master Green was able to respond, "Let me get this right. There will be other black folk like me at Cumberland Gap, like this bodyguard named Josiah? And it's not just your two sons who are feuding; the entire state of Tennessee is feuding?"

"Isaac, you are the smartest one at this table. Maybe, I should be talking to you instead," she said.

"That's an insult, Mrs. Fair," said Master Green turning cherry red.

She asked, "Have you told Isaac that there are black freedmen and black slaveholders?"

Standing again, Master Green said, "Mrs. Fair, that's enough. Why are you telling Isaac all of this now? It's not your place."

"Everything in Newton County is my business. You don't want to go off and Isaac finds out all of these things and becomes dismayed. The time to build trust is now, Abraham," she said.

I said, "Mrs. Fair, I know that blacks are free. My mother's husband of two summers is free, but he don't own no slaves. You know Momma Annabel's husband, Tunk, who is the slave driver at the Green Farm."

Master Green turned to Mrs. Fair and said, "See, I am smarter than you think. Why don't you tell me these things versus inviting Isaac to the table?"

"Well, Isaac listens and you and Marty think you know it all." She turned to Wilson and said, "Wilson, go fetch me a fan. It's hot in here."

As Wilson searched around the jail for something to fan Mrs. Fair, I asked, "Mrs. Fair, how do you know all of this information?"

"When you have been in county politics as long as my family has been in politics, you learn a great deal. I want you and Abraham to come back here in one piece."

I realized that Mr. Fair was very silent. I didn't really understand why until I noticed that he was asleep. Perhaps there was too much talk about the war and all. So, I asked Mrs. Fair, "What advice do you have for me? I don't want no trouble."

"That's a good question. Newton County has been training you for this day Isaac all your life. We in the county knew that slavery wasn't going to last always. I want you to come back a leader. Help us rebuild this community. Leaders don't wait until trouble comes; they strategize for years about how to withstand the worst of circumstances." She looked at me to see if I understood what she was saying. Then Wilson passed her a piece of parchment that he folded back and forth several times into a throwaway fan.

I said, "Mrs. Fair, we've been living together as blacks, whites, and reds in this county for years. Sure, some people don't want the slave to progress, but I don't listen because I want to own a house and land of my own one day. I don't know if I'll be staying in Newton County."

She looked dismayed, and I felt bad for telling her my plans. Then she said, "Isaac, you need to know something else."

"What is it, Mrs. Fair?"

"When President Abraham Lincoln heard firsthand the intelligent words from Frederick Douglass, Lincoln realized that his world had already changed. We in the Deep South knew all the time that black people are cut from the same board of cloth as whites. That's why Sally has been teaching all of your family to read and write, and why Abraham takes you to all of his business meetings. He has been training you how to conduct business for yourself. However, there are people from both the north and the south who still want to keep the slaves oppressed."

I asked, "Well then Mrs. Fair, why am I being held down now?"

Master Green interrupted and said, "I told you Isaac. It's because of the laws in the state of Georgia. That's why I can't set you free or I will go to jail. Then what will you and your family do?"

"So why is President Lincoln causing the people to fight each other? Shouldn't he be fighting in the courtrooms to change the laws in the southern states instead of going to war?"

I asked trying to understand why Master Green couldn't set me free right then and there.

"Like I told you before, Isaac, it's complicated," he said.

Mrs. Fair said, "Here's my advice, Isaac. Don't judge a man until you hear him speak from his heart. Quite a few men will be talking big in front of others. For the most part, southern people are fair. Give them a while and they will warm up to you. Remember this night as proof."

I looked over at Wilson who was my best friend since I could barely walk. Tonight, he said some ugly things in front of others. I knew that before daybreak, he would be at the Green Farm apologizing. He and I could never stay mad for long.

She tried to stand up, but dropped heavily right back down into the chair. I hopped up from my seat and gave her a hand. For a moment, I felt as though there was only Mrs. Fair and me in the room. She possessed a way of making every citizen in Newton County feel like they were the only one who mattered—finally I was becoming one of them. After she gained her footing, she asked, "Isaac, do you know about the Gaither Plantation down the way?"

"Yes ma'am."

"You make us proud in the war. Abraham might be a farmer. I believe in my heart of hearts that you will be a rich planter one day. You remember this old lady."

I dared not reply or look back at Master Green because I knew he was turning cherry red with anger. To my surprise as he turned the knob of the jail door, Master Green said, "Mrs. Fair, for once, we agree."

Within the hour, the Atlanta Journal missed a provisional parade in Oxford. That dreary night after the rain stopped, the Oxford community through word of mouth heard the news and came out in full force to welcome us back safely into the community. Each neighbor stood out in front of their manicured lawns holding a candle. A few stars provided some light; however, the neighbors' candles lit the path back to the Green Farm. I could tell by the look on Master Green's face that he was proud to be a citizen of Oxford.

As the two horses trotted across the pebble stone driveway at the Green Farm, there were also candles in the back of the house. Within minutes, I saw my entire slave family. Even Mrs. Sally was outdoors to greet us. Following Master Green and me back to the stables, she asked, "Abraham, are you and Isaac alright? They didn't hurt him, did they?"

"No dear. The matter is settled," he said dismounting Sunlight.

"Good."

As I dismounted Daybreak, Rosa Lee embraced me. Then Momma Annabel and my four brothers, Jeremiah, Frank, and the twins, Alfred and Wilfred, each gave me a warm hug. With the exception of Jeremiah, my younger brothers all lived to see at least 16 or more winters and were born only a year or two apart.

My mother's husband, Tunk, walked out of Momma Annabel's slave house, shook my hand, and said in a baritone voice, "Boy, you scared your mother half to death." I wasn't expecting a warm welcome from him because his role was that of the slave driver and disciplinarian. One thing was for sure, Tunk was not our biological father because none of us looked like him. We all favored our mother. However, we respected him just the same.

Because the hour was so late, I could see the disappointment in Rosa Lee's eyes that she and I would not be able to spend quality time together before I headed off to Cumberland Gap. After we all were inside of our individual slave houses, Master Green locked us in for the evening. For the first time in my life, I didn't know if he was locking us in so that we would not escape or locking us in to protect us from harm.

In the bedroom, I immediately removed my smelly clothes and relieved myself in the porcelain bedpan. Hearing Rosa Lee sing "Beautiful Dreamer" by Stephen Foster, I knew that I was going to miss hearing Mrs. Sally and her harmonizing around the Green farmhouse.

In the adjacent room with glowing candles all around, Rosa Lee warmed the water in the fireplace for my bath. Within minutes, I relaxed in the extra long galvanized wash tub as Rosa Lee knelt down on the floor with a sponge to wash my back. She asked, "Why did Redhead Wilson snatch you up?"

"I don't rightly know. Maybe he is going to miss me when I go off to war."

Laughing, Rosa Lee said, "Next time, tell him to just come out and say that he doesn't want you to go."

"What about you? Do you want me to go?" As the water rolled down my back, I gazed into her beautiful brown eyes.

"I can't wait for you to leave so that I can have the bed to myself," she said teasing. "Do you think Master Green will keep his word and let you have his daddy's farm in Dublin?"

"Not sure."

She placed her hand in the lukewarm bath water, stood up and walked over to the fireplace to retrieve a kettle of hot water. By the time she returned from across the room, I was already standing with a towel around my waist. Rosa Lee asked, "Are you done? I'd plan for us to take a walk but now we are locked in for the night." Tears formed in her eyes, and I searched for words to say. For the slave, nothing seemed to go as planned. This time when we embraced, I wished her hug would last me for eternity. Before I could tell her a word, she already knew what I was going to say.

"Let me turn down the bed for you so that you can get a good night's sleep before your journey to Big Shanty in the morning," she said with a slight smile.

Chapter 5

MOMMA ANNABEL'S PRAYERS sounded throughout the slave quarters, and I woke up from a peaceful sleep. Through the window, a triangular bit of sunlight shone on the wooden floor. When I turned in the bed, Rosa Lee was not there. So, I slipped on my grey drawstring pants, reached under the bed, and pulled out the porcelain bedpan.

Heading out the door, I walked between the two rows of houses towards the pea field where there was a wooden outhouse with two separate doors, one side for the Greens and one for the slaves. Because Master Green took pride in Georgian architecture, the outhouse was painted white and looked like a tiny replicate of his farmhouse. To say the scent of the outhouse was unpleasant is an understatement. Therefore, I rushed to empty the bedpan and quickly closed the outhouse door.

As I faced the front door of my brothers' slave houses, I decided not to wake them up so early in the morning. The golden sun was midway across the horizon as the black and white spotted cows grazed the green grass in the distance while the chickens clucked in the nearby chicken coop. Smelling the pigpen towards the left, I knew that Jeremiah would be out to slop the hogs soon.

By the time I entered the backdoor of my slave house, I returned the bedpan under the bed and was pleasantly surprised that Rosa Lee already heated the water for me to wash my hands in the galvanized tin bucket.

When I turned around, Rosa Lee opened the front door with a breakfast tray. The country ham and eggs smelled wonderful, and I wondered if the Confederate States Army served the soldiers a hot breakfast every morning. She wore one of Mrs. Sally's purple designer dresses, and I wished that I possessed a drawing of her to carry with me to war.

Wearing a white drop shoulder shirt and bleached white cloth diaper, Baby Jacob began to cry, and Rosa Lee said, "I will calm him down. You eat up."

"You know I love to hold our baby. Have you eaten yet?"

Picking up Jacob from his bed, she said, "I ate as I cooked. You aren't going to wear those dingy pants, are you?"

"I can dress myself." Opening up the mahogany wooden chest at the foot of the bed, I retrieved a white linen shirt with black cotton pants as well as my best pair of brown boots.

Then there was a knock on the front door, and Master Green said, "You ready to go? It will take about three to four days to get to Big Shanty, Georgia from Oxford. Go on and give Rosa Lee your good-bye kisses so we can go."

Standing at the threshold with tears in her eyes, she said, "You haven't eaten yet. I guess it's that time."

"Now don't you go making me sad. You said that I was going to be fine, and I will be."

As she leaned Jacob towards me, I gave him a big kiss. After Rosa Lee and I embraced, I walked out of the backdoor and cut a right turn to head over to the stables. I noticed that Master Green was wearing a plain white cotton shirt, brown pants and a new pair of black boots.

When he saw that I was mounting Daybreak, he said, "You are going to ride Midnight. We aren't taking Daybreak."

I said, "You want to go and get me killed before I pick up the first military issued rifle? Midnight is afraid of field mice. How is he going to deal with the sound of gunfire?"

"There will be more than gunfire. There will be cannons and explosions."

"All the more reason to take Daybreak," I said sitting in the saddle ready to leave the farm.

"Daybreak is too old. Midnight and Sunlight can be trained well at Camp McDonald with all of the other horses," he said lifting up Midnight's hind leg to show me the horse's strong muscle. He added, "So get on down from there."

"With all due respect, I am not going to war and get killed from falling off of a horse. How crazy would that be? He almost trampled over me last night from the thunder."

"You are not emancipated yet. I said get off of that horse." Standing in front of Daybreak, Master Green's face turned cherry red. When he saw the determination in my eyes, he added, "By the way, did you give Rosa Lee her goodbye present?"

Dismounting Daybreak, I said, "No, I forgot. Give me a few minutes."

I walked back towards the slave courtyard. Underneath the crawlspace on the left side of my slave house was Rosa Lee's present in an uncovered small pine wooden box. When I entered through the backdoor, I saw that she was in the bedroom sitting in a rocking chair with Jacob. Standing at the door, I said, "I forgot to give you something."

She asked "What do we have here?" Then she stood to place Jacob in his bed, reached for her gift, and said, "Isaac, I love her."

"Him," I said passing her the chocolate Labrador Retriever puppy.

"Will he harm Jacob? I don't want a mean dog," she said stroking his soft brown coat.

"I wouldn't give you a gift that would hurt you or Jacob. About three days ago, I did some extra work for Master Green; and he gave me some vegetables to trade Redhead Wilson for the puppy. We thought that a dog will keep you company while I am away."

She entered into the adjourning room and reached for the pitcher of water and a small bowl. I think she was extremely disappointed that the puppy would not take a drink.

Then there was a knock on the front door. I sighed knowing that Master Green and I still needed to resolve the matter about Daybreak.

Outside standing with his hands in his pockets, Wilson was wearing tan work pants, a white shirt and black suspenders. Red Georgia clay was all over his work boots. He said, "May I speak to you for a moment? I have to hurry because Mr. Fair doesn't know that I'm here."

Unsure if I was coming back into the house, I gave Rosa Lee a kiss on the forehead and said, "Alright."

Wilson and I walked to the right towards the kitchen house, but I dared not go in because of all the knives inside. I didn't know how this talk was going to turn out.

He said, "Isaac, I want to apologize about yesterday. You are like a brother to me."

Though there was not one tear in his eyes, I knew that he was sincere. So, I said, "Don't pay that no never mind. I know that Mr. Fair and his boys put you up to it. He was going to whip you for sure if you didn't do what he said. When I got back home last night, I wondered if I would have taken a beaten for you if the tables were turned. I probably would have done the same thing."

"I didn't mean what I said about Jacob either. The reason I came over is to offer Rosa Lee some help with Jacob while you are away at Cumberland Gap. I want to teach him how to play ball like we did with Jeremiah . . . since we don't know how long you will be gone."

"Rosa Lee would like your help, but Jacob won't be walking for a while."

He laughed and said, "That's why I'm making the offer."

With my right hand, I patted him on his left shoulder and said, "When you said last night that you were going to buy Jacob, to tell you the truth, I was glad."

He asked, "Are you crazy?"

"I mean it; because I know that if you ever buy any of us, you would be the one to set us free."

He rubbed his fiery red hair and said, "You sure look at things in the most peculiar ways." Scanning the area to see if anyone was in the vicinity, he said, "I've been meaning to ask you this for years. There is no better time than the present. Since Tunk is a freedman, why doesn't Momma Annabel just go far away from here and live with Tunk?"

"Tunk has a piece of land in Marietta, Georgia not far from Big Shanty. When I travel with Master Green to visit Mr. Mable, his cousin in Mill Grove, we sometimes stop at Tunk's house."

"What kind of house is it?"

"Tunk calls it a four bedroom Georgian Cottage. All I know is that it is not a shotgun slave house. Momma Annabel thinks that the law will just pick her back up and sell her to some new slave master if she goes off and lives with Tunk. The only way I'm going to get her out of Oxford is if I move to Dublin, Georgia."

"Well, I was just wondering. Tunk being a black freedman and all, I ain't gonna lie to you. I envy him sometimes. He has his own house; and he is getting paid to be a slave driver for his own family. That's why you don't have one whip mark on your back. How often does he travel home to Marietta?"

"When we aren't working in the fields, he moves back to Marietta; then he comes back to Oxford. I try not to think about Tunk being free."

"I hear you. Can I help you get saddled up?"

As we walked over to the stables, Master Green smiled with approval when he saw Wilson and me together. He said, "The newspapers say that black and white don't get along in the south. Where is Harper's Weekly to draw a picture of you two in harmony on the Green Farm?"

Wilson said, "That's because they're talking to the wealthy plantation owners with hundreds of slaves and indentured servants. They ain't talking to no farmers. I never want to work on a plantation. I'll serve my time right here in the Covington area until I get my papers."

Master Green said, "You will, Wilson. You will."

When I saddled Midnight, Wilson said, "Whoa, you can't ride Midnight to Big Shanty. He is buck wild. He will throw you as soon as he hears the first gunshot."

I said, "See, Master Green, I told you that I should take Daybreak. You are old and you are going to Cumberland Gap." We all laughed, and I was glad that things were back to normal—as far as normal goes for a slave.

As Master Green and I rode on the horses down the pebble stone driveway, Wilson, Jeremiah, Frank, Alfred, Wilfred, Momma Annabel and Mrs. Sally stood in the front yard and waved farewell. Tunk was nowhere in sight. Once Master Green and I were on the Georgia red dirt road, I looked back and saw Rosa Lee running down the road blowing kisses.

Camp McDonald at Big Shanty, Georgia

(March 1862-April 1862)

Chapter **6**

AS WE APPROACHED Big Shanty, Georgia, on the 10th instant, not a single cloud was in the clear blue March sky. I did not know what to expect during training at Camp McDonald. This was my first extended trip away from home. A cluster of white tepee tents could be seen from a distance. There was a manly scent in the air that could not be explained. Then I wondered if we would be able to bathe on a daily basis.

Before I could dismount Midnight, a senior enlisted soldier said, "Black rebels are not allowed."

As I swung my right leg over the horse and planted my feet on the ground, I said, "The only color I know is rebel grey."

Several men laughed. Never looking me directly in the eyes, the senior enlisted soldier said, "Oh I see, you one of them good coons."

You would have thought that Master Green was in the direct line of fire. As he dismounted Sunlight, Master Green shouted, "No one, but no one, speaks to Isaac like that! He never has eaten raccoon and never will eat raccoon." He took a deep breath and added, "If any of you lay a hand on Issac, I'll kill you myself." As Master Green waved his hand in the air, I thought he would have a heart attack right then and there. However, he continued and said, "Isaac is with me. You prefer him to be contraband?"

The senior enlisted soldier said, "Heck no, I don't want him to be contraband, one of those slaves who escapes across Union lines."

"Well then, you decide. He can stay here with me or go on up north and fight for the other side."

Turning to me, the senior enlisted soldier asked, "What took you all so long to travel here?"

I said, "We're midnight ramblers and four day tramps." A group of field officers and company commanders who were standing around laughed.

"Which way did you travel?" he asked.

"From the east of Oxford to due west here in Big Shanty . . . Why? What shrine are you from?" I asked with a smile.

Deciding to ease up a little, the senior enlisted soldier asked Master Green, "Can he read? Right now our regiment needs a chaplain."

Master Green said, "No, he can't read, but he has memorized almost every word in the *Bible.* Also, he serves as the minister every 4th Sunday at the Methodist Episcopal Church South in Oxford."

"They don't allow any slaves to minister at the Methodist Episcopal Church South."

"Oh yes they do. Bishop Andrew and others minister on the 1st, 2nd, and 3rd Sunday. On the 4th Sunday, Isaac here ministers; and whosoever will let him come."

"Well, I'll be. Is Isaac ordained?"

"Yes, he is licensed to preach," said Master Green with one strong pat on my back.

The senior enlisted soldier frowned and said, "I bet no black ministers will be at the general conference of the Methodist Episcopal Church South in New Orleans this spring."

"Why not? There are 207,000 slaves who are members of the Methodist Episcopal Church South."

"Wait a bloody minute. We just can't allow black rebels to be ministers in the 42nd Regiment Georgia Volunteers."

"Didn't I hear of the Union Paymaster General Benjamin Larnard talk about French cooks serving as chaplains? When it comes to God, why should it matter if a rebel is light grey or dark grey?"

The officers of Company E stepped a few paces away and huddled to take a vote. While waiting, the minutes seemed like hours. I wondered if they were deciding if Master Green and I should even be enlisted with their regiment. So far, I felt extremely uncomfortable coming along with Master Green.

The senior enlisted soldier returned and said, "We just got us a chaplain." Turning to me, he said, "Go into that tent over there, fetch us a *Bible* and say something from Psalms."

The closer I reached the white tepee coned shaped tent, I felt as though every eye in the camp was on me. There were two men playing checkers at a wooden stump table. Off to my left, another man was shoeing a white American Shetland horse which was positioned close to a pony carriage. After seeing the *Bible* just inside of the tent, I came back towards the senior enlisted soldier and Master Green while I flipped through the pages of the *Bible*.

"Why don't you read to these fine gentlemen Psalm 20:7?" asked Master Green with a quick wink.

After I cleared my throat, I read, "Some trust in chariots, and some in horses, but we will remember the name of the Lord our God."

The senior enlisted soldier smirked and asked, "Well, what you got to say about that Chaplain Issac?"

I noticed a group of men gathering around me, and I said, "Well sir, every man out here has left their homes and family. The future is quite uncertain." As I watched across the field, even more men were walking at a slow pace towards me. Though I never witnessed a lynching personally, I read articles in the Southern Confederacy newspaper about men being strung from a tree for the smallest infractions. I felt that I must think fast or perhaps Master Green would not be able to hold back an angry mob for a black rebel being at the camp. So, I said, "We do not know what lies ahead of us during this journey. What we do know is that we cannot trust anyone but God Himself. Let us pray."

As I bowed my head, I felt a hand rest gently on the back of my left shoulder. I don't know where the words for this prayer abounded; however, from the warmth of the person's hand, I felt a sense of community that I had never felt before in the Deep South. When I opened my eyes, men were connected hand to shoulder for what appeared to be yards and yards. Some men even had tears in their eyes. Confidently, I said, "Don't worry about what you have left behind. We look towards the hills from wench cometh our help . . . our help cometh from the Lord."

As the senior enlisted soldier looked out across his band of soldiers, in unison they said, "So mote it be."

Then the senior enlisted soldier looked me in the eyes for the first time and said, "Thanks Chaplain Isaac. The men have been praying for your arrival."

As the crowd dispersed, Master Green turned to me and said, "Isaac, why don't you go and take the horses to the stables. I don't believe that I've properly introduced myself."

"Well, I am quite speechless after that spiritual prayer. I did not mean you no disrespect. I'm Sergeant Major Hart. And you are?" he asked with an outreached hand.

"I'm Abraham Green. I own a small farm on the outskirts of Atlanta, Georgia," he said shaking the senior enlisted soldier's hand.

"We have been here since the 4th instant. You are late. Have you properly enlisted?"

"Yes, here are my papers. I am waiting to receive the $50 bounty and $25 for clothing. My previous rank in the United States military was Sergeant Major, so this is how I've enlisted for this tour of duty."

As Sergeant Major Hart thumbed through some papers, he said, "I have you right here. Wait a minute. How in the world did you enlist Isaac?"

"When I went to the courthouse, I told them that Isaac was joining me so they enlisted him too. I was quite surprised myself; however, I knew the money would come in handy for our travels here to Camp McDonald."

"Well, we have a problem," said Sergeant Major Hart.

"What could that possibly be?"

"We don't have any separate tents for black rebels. He is the first to even step foot at Camp McDonald as an enlisted soldier."

"Well, then that will not be a problem because he will be in my assigned tent."

"I cannot approve such an outlandish idea."

"I see it this way. The slave is considered property in the south. Right?"

"Right."

"Well, I'm sleeping in the same tent with my property . . . end of story."

By the look on Sergeant Major Hart's red face, I could tell that Master Green was putting his foot down about something. The two men were bantering back and forth until I wondered if I should even tie up the horses. Perhaps our journey was already over. The crowd, which was a few moments ago at peace, started to move back towards Sergeant Major Hart. I knew that I needed to think quickly again or the situation would get out of hand. So, I hightailed back over to the senior enlisted soldier and said, "Sir, the men are getting restless. Is it time for noon day lunch?"

Before Master Green could reprimand me for interrupting his conversation with Sergeant Major Hart, the senior enlisted soldier saw the crowd approaching from his left and said, "Chaplain Isaac, that's a good idea."

Master Green asked Sergeant Major Hart, "What's it going to be?"

"You are putting me in a very strange predicament," said Sergeant Major Hart. Facing the crowd Sergeant Major Hart said, "Soldiers, let me introduce to you Sergeant Major Abraham Green and Chaplain Isaac who hail from Oxford, Georgia. Because we are tight on space here at this training camp, I have invited them both to stay in the officer's quarters."

"Permission to speak Sergeant Major," said a First Sergeant at the front of the crowd.

"Permission granted."

"I am First Sergeant Russell. This is the war of the Confederate States of America. Only one-tenth of the people in this state own slaves . . . and for the most part that's the planters. As for the men in my tent, we don't own any slaves. Have you read the latest Harper's Weekly newspaper?" he asked pulling out a torn sheet.

"What does an article have to do with where Sergeant Major Green and Chaplain Isaac sleep?"

"Let me read to you an article from Harper's Weekly newspaper." Lifting the newspaper clipping and shouting to the top of his authoritative voice for the seventy-six men of the 42nd Regiment Georgia Volunteers Company E to hear, he said, "The correspondent of the New York Herald, in one of its late numbers, reports that the rebels had a regiment of mounted black men armed with sabers at Manassas, and that some five hundred Union prisoners taken at Bull Run were escorted to their filthy prison by a regiment of black men."

The 42nd Regiment Georgia Volunteers Company E cheered.

Master Green winked at me and smiled.

Sergeant Major Hart asked, "What's your point?"

First Sergeant Russell said, "If these black rebels can fight for the honor of the Confederacy, I don't see why our chaplain can't be living amongst the soldiers. After the prayer, we in Company E took a vote, we want Chaplain Isaac to be assigned to our company and be assigned to my tent."

Listening to this news was baffling to me. Learning from the First Sergeant, I asked, "Permission to speak, sir."

"Yes, Chaplain Isaac."

"Did I just hear that there are black rebels riding horses for the Confederacy?"

"Well, Harper's Weekly states that the New York Herald newspaper gave that report."

"Did I also hear that a regiment of black rebels took 500 Union soldiers to a Confederate prison?"

"I am with you, Chaplain Isaac. I heard the same thing."

Master Green said, "This can't be true. Jeff Davis has not given the order for black soldiers to fight in the Confederacy."

Sergeant Major Hart said, "Sounds like your courthouse and other courthouses in the south are enlisting black rebels just the same. Look at this. The enlistment on this report just says Isaac Green. No one would ever know from this paper that Isaac is a black rebel."

Master Green said, "I'll be. I agreed for Isaac to be a chaplain because I didn't think he could fight. Isaac is the best rider in Newton County. If you boys want to win this war, I suggest that Isaac be assigned to the mounted cavalry because we will need skilled riders to travel the rugged terrains at Cumberland Gap."

First Sergeant Russell added, "Yeah, but we can't force Chaplain Isaac to fight because look at this." The soldier pulled out another clipping from Harper's Weekly. "This shows a picture of a Confederate captain pointing a gun and making two slaves load a cannon."

Master Green said, "That's propaganda. No one wants to believe that there are some areas in the south were whites and blacks get along fine. I'm not saying it's perfect for Isaac. I am saying that loyalty delivers a great prize."

First Sergeant Russell said, "Regardless, in the 42nd Regiment, we have to work together, and every man has to want to fight in this battle. What do you say Chaplain Isaac?"

Chapter 7

THE SEVENTY-SIX SOLDIERS in Company E, Master Green, and Sergeant Major Hart were left standing in the crowd. I said, "The way I see it. I don't have to fight in this war. President Lincoln is talking about emancipation, and Master Green promised me a house and land in a small town called Dublin if I get him back home to Oxford alive. My job is to protect Master Green."

Sergeant Major Hart removed his tan wide cuff gloves, smacked them in his left hand, and said, "How about this Chaplin Isaac? Train with us and then decide."

Somehow I knew that there was no choice in the matter for me. I never heard of neither a slave nor an enlisted soldier being asked to do anything. However, if he was giving me a choice like a man, then I was going to milk this opportunity for all it was worth.

As the crowd dispersed again, I was starved and asked, "When are we going to eat?"

Sergeant Major Hart said, "Well, the soldiers are getting in line now to eat corn bread, some pork skins, and coffee."

"That's it?" I asked expecting the southern cooking that I enjoyed back at the Green Farm.

Master Green said, "Well Isaac, it will have to make do for now."

"I'll go check on the horses, and then I'll get something to eat." Once I reached my horse, I pulled out my knapsack.

Inside were some chicken and biscuits that a slave family gave to me as we travelled on the long journey from Oxford to Big Shanty. After strolling several yards away from the crowd, I sat down underneath a huge hickory tree to eat my lunch. I suspected the men thought that I was being respectful by not eating with them. The sweet juice from the chicken drumstick was a reminder of the life I left behind. However, no one could cook like my Rosa Lee. Afterwards, I reached back into my knapsack and pulled out some pound cake. If pork skins were all the rations we were going to get, I just assumed to go back to Oxford and forfeit having a place of my own.

Over the next few hours, I pretty much stayed to myself. Not wanting to cause a scene, I gave some thought to being a soldier in this army. Then Master Green walked up to me and said, "I need to share something with you. I've been told that the north doesn't have the same skills in riding horses like we do in the south. I know that you aren't too keen on fighting. After some of the things that Sergeant Major Hart told me, I'm not sure if I want to fight either."

Was I hearing Master Green correctly? Why was he asking me to fight? After all, I'm the slave. Not understanding what caused the dynamics to change all of a sudden, my heart started to beat fast; and I started to perspire.

Master Green asked, "Isaac, are you alright?"

"I don't rightly know if I'm alright or not. Why you being so nice to me all of a sudden? Why are you giving me so many choices? My head hurts; that's all."

"Isaac, I've been nice to you since the day you were born. Sure, I tell you what to do and when to do it, but you have got to come to terms with our situation here. I don't want to die in this war. They tell me that Cumberland Gap is a passage through the treacherous mountain range. There aren't enough wide paths cut through these mountains for wagons and artillery. You are here because I know you are physically fit from working around the farm, and I've seen how you can handle the most spirited horse, even Midnight."

There was no need for me to answer because a slave learns to listen. A master will tell you that he "saw" the mountain. However, a slave will always tell you that he "has seen" the mountain because the slave speaks from past experience of being in the midst of all the action. So when a slave says, "I seen the mountain," know that he wasn't at the base of the mountain looking up. He was once standing on the mountain; and somehow by the grace of God, he has returned and is now standing beside his master with his feet firmly planted on the ground.

I dared not look him in the eyes as a sign of respect. However, just as I suspected, I saw his shadow leave; and when I looked up, he was headed back towards camp. Wanting to go back to Oxford, I missed Rosa Lee. I was so excited about leaving town to see what was on the other side that I didn't realize that I was going to be the only slave in this godforsaken camp. Where was this Josiah bodyguard? Then out of nowhere came First Sergeant Russell.

"Chaplain Isaac, why are you sitting over here by yourself? I want to introduce you to the men in my tent. I'm Jonathan Russell," he said extending his hand.

"Master Russell, I can't shake your hand. There are rules in the south. Where are you from?"

"I'm from Newtonsborough, and don't call me Master Russell. Call me Jonathan."

"Well, I can't do that."

"Why not?"

"I'm a slave. Why you being so nice to me anyhow? You want me to fight to save your life too?"

"How old are you, Chaplain Isaac?"

"Master Green says that I'm twenty-two years old."

"Well, I'm twenty-one. I don't give a dash what those old farts think about me talking to you. My family isn't rich enough to own no slaves. They are lying to you if you think this war is about slavery. What I'm about to tell you is on the square. Okay?"

"You mean to tell me that we are on the level?"

From the smile on his face, you would have thought First Sergeant Russell struck yellow gold. I decided to take my chances and look him in his eyes. First Sergeant Russell was about six feet tall with dirty blond hair. His eyes were green and his skin was pale. He wore a shabby grey uniform which was torn at his right knee. I asked, "If the war ain't about slavery then where are all of the slaves?"

Sitting down beside me, he said, "See that's the thing; there are black men here. They are just working. Some serve as cooks, teamsters, and some even serve as musicians. Did you know that the Confederate States Army pays a black musician the same wages as a white musician? It's written in the law."

"Do say?" I asked moving to add distance between us.

First Sergeant Russell smirked and said, "Sergeant Major Green must really treat you differently than most slaveholders because no slave has come up through the front gate before with his master. How did you learn to read?"

I chuckled and said, "Why do you think I can read? Like Master Green said, I memorized the *Bible*."

"No, I saw your eyes moving. You were reading alright. God sent you here Chaplain Isaac to show the men that the slave isn't as dumb as they think."

"How many slaves have you seen hanging from a tree?"

"None."

"Pray tell, are you lying to me?"

"I have seen men ride out into the night as if they were cowboys. Where they go and why they go, I don't ask."

"You ain't one of those snakes in the grass; are you?"

"I'm saying that every man at this camp is like family. The north has the upper hand. They have better transportation, military equipment and the backing of the United States military. Every man here at Camp McDonald is probably fighting for a different reason."

"Why's that?"

"I bet your Master Green is fighting because he heard that the Union Army is likely to take over Cumberland Gap, head straight through Atlanta and on over to Oxford."

Laughing I said, "You got that one right. So why are you here?"

"I'm a young farmer and heard that the north has established an elaborate tax system. If I don't fight, I'll have to give the government more money than I'm willing to pay or risk losing my farm. Taxation without representation is downright wrong. I didn't get a vote," he said resting his arms on his bent knees.

"Do say?"

"Then you have other men here who believe that the original intent of our founding fathers was for each individual state to have its own separate government. They call it states rights. Crazy huh?"

As I looked back towards the tents, I noticed that no one was paying First Sergeant Russell and me any attention. "I suppose."

"Do I smell some southern chicken?"

"You want a piece?"

"Sakes alive, yeah," he said taking a drumstick out of the brown woven basket.

"So what do I call you? First Sergeant Russell?"

"Let's see. We have to be very smart about how you address me as not to incite the men who do not associate with black men. However, I don't want you to call me Master either."

"Well, what's your first name?" I asked thinking hard.

"Jonathan, but they call me Johnny."

"I'll call you Johnny Rebel."

Laughing and slapping his right thigh, He said, "I'd like that. Why don't we just make it Johnny Reb for short? Do you play checkers or chess?"

"I play checkers every Sunday under a great big Georgia oak tree with the other slave men. Why?"

"Well, tonight after supper, me and the other men usually play a game of checkers or chess. You are welcome to join us."

"I don't think that would be wise. I'll just entertain myself or be with the cooks and teamsters."

"Suit yourself," he said taking the last bite of chicken.

Then I heard a big "BOOM." As I jumped up to run, Johnny Reb grabbed my left arm and said, "Slow down, Chap Issac. That's the artillerymen practicing on the smoothbore cannons. Let me show you."

As we walked a distance, there was silence between us. I made sure to keep a few paces behind Johnny Reb. However, he constantly said to me, "Come on, Chap Isaac. You have to keep up the pace because you keep falling behind."

Boom, Boom, Boom sounded the bronze cannon. A member of the platoon said, "First Sergeant Russell, who do we have here?"

"This is Chaplain Isaac from Oxford, Georgia. He is accompanying Sergeant Major Green. Since he is going with us to Cumberland Gap, why don't you tell him about the artillery section of the platoon?"

"You can't be serious? You want me to tell a black rebel about the artillery section?"

With a smirk, Johnny Reb took out his clipping of Harper's Weekly and read it to the men who were standing around the cannon.

"I'll be," said the member of the platoon. "Black rebels took Union prisoners?"

Johnny Reb said, "Yep, they took not one, not two, but 500. The way I see it, we can fight this war alone and die or do like the smart leaders in the Confederacy and use all of our resources."

The member of the platoon was silent. I could tell that he was giving this much thought. The other men seemed to be in deep thought as well. As not to start any trouble, I turned to walk away. Just as before, Johnny Reb said, "Slow down, Chap Isaac." Then he turned to the men around the cannon and said, "Give me a minute with the chaplain."

As we walked a few paces away, he said, "Let me tell you a thing about negotiating. Never move or say a word until the other man speaks. The first one who moves looses."

This was all new to me and all of these facts and figures were coming at me too fast. I held my head which pounded.

Johnny Reb continued, "Let me put it another way. I know you were sent by God, Chap Isaac. When I tore out this newspaper clipping, I had no idea that I would be standing beside you. Then to top it all off, I put the clipping in my pocket. What are the chances of that happening?"

When he realized that I was not responding, he said, "Come on back over to the cannon. Let me do the talking. You just stand there. Put your shoulders back. No, no, like this . . ."

By the time we got back to the cannon, the member of the platoon said, "I ain't having it. I don't care how many black rebels are in those other camps. We don't have no black rebels here in Big Shanty. That's the way it has been and that's the way it will always be."

Pushing the member of the platoon to the side, Johnny Reb looked at me and said, "Chap Issac, this fine gentleman here is the artillery sergeant. His name is Sergeant Brady. When we go to Cumberland Gap, his platoon includes just three men in total: a commander to give the order, a gunner and a driver. Got it?"

I said, "There are three men. Got it."

Artillery Sergeant Brady's face turned a bright red. He rolled up his sleeves, and I thought he was going to sock Johnny Reb. When the other men took a step back, I kept my eyes on Sergeant Brady while walking backwards. I didn't know if the cannon was loaded.

Artillery Sergeant Brady said, "Chaplain Isaac, get back over here. This First Sergeant don't know a thing about the artillery section. In an artillery section, there is the cannon." Then he stressed every single number as he spoke. "There are two corporals, six gunners, and six drivers. Come over here and let me show you how we load the cannon. Here, hold the sponge and the rammer."

All of the men started to laugh at the fear of terror on my face. Then Johnny Reb said, "Chap Isaac and everybody freeze." Then Johnny Reb pulled back out the cartoon in Harper Weekly's magazine of the confederate captain forcing two slaves to load a cannon. He continued, "Look at this here. This is proof that black rebels are fighting in this war. However, I think we shouldn't terrorize Chap Isaac or these newspaper reporters are going to make the Confederacy look like a bunch of racist. Let's give them a real story about how we get along at Big Shanty."

This time, I didn't move a limb as Johnny Reb spoke about how important the image of the Confederacy was to winning the war.

Artillery Sergeant Brady held the cartoon and said, "I don't rightly know anything about newspaper reporters. Why should I care what they think of the Confederacy? My job is to shoot the enemy."

Johnny Reb went on for about nine minutes or so explaining how every man at Big Shanty held a special role in the army. To be frank, I really got tired of the bickering, picked up the rammer and said, "Now what do I do?"

Chapter 8

AT 5:45 THE next morning, I was startled by the *First Call* of a bugle. Lying down on the hard ground, I noticed that my feet were to the center of the tepee tent almost touching the pole. All thirteen of us were positioned in this manner in a circle. The previous night was a blur because I was so worn out from marching around Camp McDonald. I sat up and tried my best to find Master Green amongst the men. Then the bugle sounded *Reveille.*

Johnny Reb said, "Up and at 'em. It's time for roll call."

The men started to stir and I said, "Where is Master Green?"

"He took one look at this hard ground and hightailed it to the officer's quarters. I told him that I would look after you."

Not knowing if I should be angry for being separated from Master Green or elated for the bond that was beginning to form between me and Johnny Reb, I stood, stretched and said, "How much did he pay you?"

Still lying down, another soldier in the tent chimed in and said, "Yeah, how much did he pay you?"

"An agreement between two gentlemen is a sacred trust," said Johnny Reb putting on his worn out uniform. He added, "We need to patch up the cap of this Sibley tent before bad weather comes through later this week." I looked up at the center of the Indian styled tent and saw a round piece of canvas with a long tear.

As I walked out, there was a navy blue flag trimmed in red fringe flying from a pole yards away from our tent. At the center was an arch with three pillars and a ribbon interwoven in between each column. Pointing, I asked, "What is that flag? I've never seen it before."

Joining me outside, Johnny Reb said, "That's the Georgia State Regimental Flag, which identifies to regiments from other states at Cumberland Gap that we are from the state of Georgia. As I understand it, we are going to see several varieties of regimental flags when we are off to Tennessee."

In the distance, I saw a flag with three large stripes: two red and a white stripe in the middle. In the corner there was a circle of stars on a dark blue square. Johnny Reb continued and said, "That's the national flag of the Confederate States of America."

I said, "Yeah, I know. I thought that they replaced that flag with another one that has a big X. In Oxford, I saw a new flag."

Johnny Reb said, "That X is a St. Andrew's Cross."

"Do say?"

"The St. Andrew's Cross represents humility because Andrew, the disciple of Jesus, refused to be crucified on the same wooden cross formation as Jesus. Do you know the history of why the battle flag was created?"

"I heard that because the United States flag and the Confederate States of America national flag look so much alike on the battlefield, both sides were getting confused."

"As a matter of fact, I think that Confederate General Ben McCulloch got the two flags confused during the Battle of Pea Ridge because he emerged from some bushes right in front of the Union lines and was killed."

"Do say? I thought that I would see just the battle flag."

Johnny Reb smiled and said, "No, you are going to see lots of flags. However, General Beauregard insists that the flag with the St. Andrew's Cross be used on the battlefield."

"We call the Confederate States of America national flag the stars and bars."

"I thought the battle flag was the stars and bars."

"Nope, the national flag is called the stars and bars."

"Johnny Reb, I think I like the Georgia State Regimental Flag the best. Why is there a building with pillars that remind me of the story of Sampson in the *Bible*?"

"You are in luck. I do know what that means. The three pillars represent justice, wisdom, and moderation."

I smirked and said, "Johnny Reb, I ain't never met anyone like you before."

"What do you mean?"

"You talk like a book."

"Well, I want to be a journalist one day. So, I study all kinds of facts. I am going to work for a national newspaper."

"Are you going to move to Gotham?"

"Why would I move to New York? There are plenty of newspaper companies in the south." Annoyed, he turned to line up Company E for roll call.

After receiving instructions for the day, all the men proceeded to their designated drilling areas. However, Johnny Reb asked me to follow him. Thinking he was still agitated by my Gotham comment, I kept a close eye on Johnny Reb's hands.

As we walked towards the stables, Johnny Reb said, "Before I introduce you to your post with the mounted cavalry, there are some things you need to know."

"I think Master Green has told me everything I need to know months before coming to this war." Stopping a few feet short of the stables, I could see Midnight and Sunlight with the other horses.

"I have told the other men that I'm going to give you a tour of Camp McDonald so they don't know about this conversation. You have to hear me Chap Isaac and hear me good."

With a concerned look on my face, I said, "What's on your mind?"

As to be convincing to the others, Johnny Reb pointed out the nearby cornfield and garden. Then he said, "You are in Cobb County."

"Yes, I know."

"It is also important to know that this county is named for Thomas W. Cobb, the cousin of Thomas R.R. Cobb."

As I looked to my left, there were mounted cavalrymen drilling on the parade ground. I assumed that this was going to be a very short tour. However, Johnny Reb turned to the right and passed the artillery battalion. I said, "Master Green talks about Thomas R.R. Cobb, a big time politician who played a major part in the south seceding."

Because of the cannons firing, I could barely hear what Johnny Reb was saying which is why I picked up my pace to remain by his side. So, we walked until we were at the front of the camp where he pointed out the Western and Atlantic Railroad. He said, "You being a minster and all, do you know about Thomas R.R. Cobb's legal writings which justify slavery?"

"At times, we talk about it during 4th Sunday church services in Oxford. Thomas R.R. Cobb and others believe slavery is justified because of the *Bible's* account of 'The Curse of Ham.'"

Heading towards the front, Johnny Reb said, "That's the Lacy Hotel across the railroad tracks. Can you smell the flapjacks?"

"No, I smell the bacon." There were a group of people dressed in business attire coming out of the hotel. I continued, "Some folk in the south believe that because Noah's son, Ham, saw Noah naked that Noah cursed the descendents of Ham's son, Canaan, to be servants for generations to come."

"Right . . . Many men here will believe Thomas R.R. Cobb's belief that Africans are Ham's descendents, and Africans were destined to be slaves."

"Johnny Reb, Master Green isn't buying 'The Curse of Ham' theory." Continuing to walk adjacent to the tracks across from the Lacy Hotel, I saw the rifle area on the west side of the camp.

Taking out his journalist pad and quill, Johnny Reb asked, "What does Sergeant Major Green think slavery is about?"

"Have you ever heard of indentured servants?"

Leading me to a table not far from a second parade ground, he said, "Have a seat and let's talk about it. My father was an involuntary indentured servant; however, I was born free. What in the world does slavery have to do with indentured servitude?"

Sitting down on the wooden table bench across from Johnny Reb, I said, "Years ago, several different races tilled the land in these Confederate States and worked the fields. No doubt these people wanted more money for working the fields than the planters, like Thomas R.R. Cobb, were willing to pay."

"I'm listening," he said licking the tip of his quill.

Leaning on the table, I rested my thumb underneath my chin with my fingers extended up and my palm facing him. I said, "Because the planters did not want to pay the high wages, they looked for cheaper labor in other countries around the world. They found the solution in Africa."

"That's balderdash!" exclaimed Johnny Reb.

"It is not foolishness. Slavery is the solution to high cost labor because other races, like the Irish, Dutch, and French, demanded more money to work in the fields."

Sounding like a journalist, he asked, "So, you don't believe that 'The Curse of Ham' has anything to do with slavery?"

"Sure 'The Curse of Ham' has been used as a platform to justify slavery. I'm not naive. People misinterpret the *Bible* all the time. Religious convictions are the hardest to overcome. What's your point about Thomas R.R. Cobb?"

Sounding like a comrade, he said, "Don't mention President Jefferson Davis at this camp." Out of nowhere, an insect zoomed past, and Johnny Reb jumped off the bench.

I said, "Don't mind that carpenter bee. He won't sting you."

After Johnny Reb settled back down on the bench, he continued, "Like I was saying, don't mention Jeff Davis at this camp."

"Why not, I thought the Confederates loved Jeff Davis. Heck, some of the neighboring slaves in Oxford call me a Jeff Davis man because I came here with Master Green."

"Thomas R.R. Cobb is blaming Jeff Davis for the Confederates loosing the battles in this war."

"That's not all I heard. Master Green says that Thomas R.R. Cobb is upset for not receiving a military promotion in the Confederate States Army. Thomas R.R. Cobb believes if he were general we would be winning against the Union."

"Are you mad at Thomas R.R. Cobb for his legislation to keep slavery alive?"

"I don't know if I like him or not, I ain't met him yet."

Scribbling down my every word, Johnny Reb said, "You sure know plenty about political matters."

"I'm known in Oxford as a good listener."

"All I'm saying is to be very careful about what you say in these parts. That's all."

"There is one thing a slave learns and that is not to talk about the big bugs. Johnny Reb, where are you from?"

"When my father was an indentured servant, we lived in Augusta, Georgia; however, after his servitude we moved to Newtonsborough.

"No, I mean; where is your family originally from?"

"The Netherlands, I'm Dutch."

"How do you feel about slavery?" I asked wanting to know if I should trust a man whom I barely knew.

"Like I said, I don't own any slaves. I'm here because my father gave me a track of land in Mansfield. I believe if the Union wins that the taxes on my property are going up immensely. Then, I'll have to pay more than I have to give or lose my farmland. No offense, the planters are not going to assume the total burden of a tax increase because of slave property. Some of that burden is going to fall upon the young farmers, like me."

Knowing that he really didn't answer my question, I decided to judge him by his actions versus his words. Less than one week ago, I could not fathom that a man of another color would willingly teach me about the Confederate States Army.

I asked, "If most of the people here don't have slaves, then why don't they like the slave?"

"Let me ask you a question based on Sergeant Major Green's theory. If a race of people showed up today and took the jobs from you and your family, would you like them?"

"But I didn't volunteer to come to America from Africa and take their jobs."

"Ham didn't intend to see his father Noah naked either."

Chapter 9

THE SPRING SHOWERS from the last few days generated humidity that filled the air. On this 11ᵗʰ instant of April, the line for the mounted cavalrymen test was extremely long. Training vigorously for over a month, I felt as though I would at any moment faint. I tucked in my rebel grey shirt and tightened my belt to insure that I looked presentable.

With his elbows resting on the top rail and his left foot on the bottom rail of the wooden horse fence, Master Green nodded as I entered onto the Camp McDonald parade ground. To his right were a few cooks and teamsters who waved; however, I stayed focused so that I could hear every single command.

Smiling from ear to ear, a soldier led his horse out of the soggy parade ground area. After I approached Midnight from the right, I grabbed the rein and placed the left cheek of my face against his throat. Midnight nickered quietly and moved towards me to signal "hello."

Posted a few yards away in his rebel grey, Johnny Reb exclaimed, "Boots and Saddles!"

Each motion came natural to me as I raised my head high and moved to Midnight's left side. In the distance, the white apple blossom trees emanated an awful odor, and I sneezed. As I saddled Midnight, a bothersome fly was by my nose, and I tried my best not to swat because Momma Annabel said that the fly wards off evil.

"To horse!" exclaimed Johnny Reb.

Knowing that there would be about 37 calls in total, I whispered a prayer as I moved out. Later during the drill, Midnight successfully backed up, and I breathed a sigh of relief. While training, I witnessed other horses responding to Johnny Reb's commands without riders. However, Midnight refused to be an overachiever.

When the time came for the live-fire exercise, I prayed that Midnight would not flinch. So far, the horsemanship and mounted formation drills were going extremely well. When I was directed to jump the ditch and bar, my confidence soared because this was one of Midnight's strengths.

"To arms," exclaimed Johnny Reb which was my signal to dismount. In a real battle, I would turn out under arms on foot and fight like a real soldier.

Master Green walked over to Sergeant Major Hart and said with pride, "Did you see those high leaps over the ditch and the bar? I thought Isaac was St. Martin soaring to the heavens above. So, did he pass?"

Sergeant Major Hart said, "I can't officially say; but Private Green not only passed, he also broke a few Camp McDonald mounted cavalrymen records."

"I knew it! I knew it! What is his assignment?"

"Light Cavalry."

Surprisingly when I joined them, Master Green shook my hand and patted me on the back.

Turning around to Sergeant Major Hart, he asked, "Light Cavalry? That's a job for a parlor soldier. Isaac has earned his place in the Heavy Cavalry."

Exhaling deeply, Sergeant Major Hart said, "This is not your funeral. We need a scout, someone who can inform us of the Union movements and return with that assessment quickly. Private Green is just the man."

"I want Isaac to see the elephant," said Master Green shaking his index finger.

"Well, you should be grateful that Private Green isn't going into combat with our web feet."

"Our 42nd infantry officers will give Isaac a better position on the battlefield," said Master Green removing his foot from the rail of the wooden horse fence and stomping once on the ground.

"When we find a drummer, Private Green and the drummer will be essential to our communications as well as supply lines," said Sergeant Major Hart who turned his back away from Master Green to judge the next company of soldiers.

Johnny Reb ran up to me and said, "Chap Isaac, take Midnight back to the stables."

The smile on my face was evident to every mounted cavalryman at Camp McDonald when the cooks and teamsters formed a receiving line by the fence, and I shook each hand.

"So what is your assignment?" asked a cook with grey hair.

I said, "They assigned me to the Light Cavalry to scope out every move of the Union soldiers at Cumberland Gap. It's official; we were mustered earlier today."

Pushing up the wide brim of his grey hat, he said, "Pray tell, we are very proud of you. You looked mighty good out on the parade ground today."

"Why, thank you. Where are you all from?" I asked noticing that the teamsters were wearing their rebel grey uniforms while the cook was adorned in a white shirt, pants with an army apron and high black boots.

Motioning for the others to come closer, he said, "We are from different parts of Georgia. . . . From Virginia, my cousin Jeff, who is one of Major General Stonewall Jackson's cooks, wrote me a letter. Jeff said that Stonewall Jackson's personal servant, Jim, is amongst 3,000 black men with Stonewall Jackson's troops."

"Do say?" I asked wondering if the number of black men recorded had anything to do with the number of slaveholders enlisted as soldiers.

"Jeff also said that General Robert E. Lee's cook, William, was on the battle line with the General. During combat, Robert E. Lee told William to get back behind the animals . . ."

". . . the animals?" I asked scratching my temple.

"You know, behind the line of fire. Robert E. Lee knew that he'd no longer have a cook if William got killed. Sure enough, within a minute after General Lee's warning, William was shot."

"Did William give up the ghost?" I whispered trying not to draw attention to our conversation.

"No, he's doing fine now. Here is my point. Whether it's 3,000 black men or one facing the elephant, it does my heart joy to see any black man working side by side with men of a different color. History may call it a minor step in the Deep South, but it's a step still indeed," said the grey haired cook.

"That is mighty nice of you to include me in that number."

A teamster nudged the cook and said, "Tell him about Richmond."

The cook said, "Oh yeah, about this time last year, a Yankee scout reported that the Confederate Richmond Howitzer Battery was manned by blacks. Not only that, Confederate Colonel John Hunt Morgan of Kentucky has 15 mounted black men with him too." Tilting his head, the cook asked, "How did you learn to ride a horse like that?"

Glimpsing over to Master Green, I said, "I've been riding a pony since I could barely walk. When the Civil War started last year, we slaves organized a small riding militia group to protect the town of Oxford."

The cook shook my hand again and said, "I could tell that you were trained. Do you mind me sharing some advice with you, son—as a Confederate cook, of course?"

"I can use all of the help I can get," I said wondering how long Johnny Reb was going to allow me to talk before I took Midnight back to the stables.

The cook continued, "Civil War life is hard. There will come a time when you might not have any rations to eat. You will be asked to forage for food."

"Do say? What is forage?"

"Forage means to go hunting for something to eat so that you and the other men won't starve to death. I hear that some soldiers steal from the mouths of women and children to find enough grub for their regiments. Did you leave a family home, son?"

"Yes sir, I did."

"When times get hard, you think of your family before taking food from those wives and children whose husbands and fathers left them behind. You do the right thing when you go off to war."

"Sir, I will."

Mounting, I heard Midnight snort, and I asked, "What's wrong boy?"

Shouting reverberated from the vicinity of Johnny Reb. A private who must have tasted too much of that oil of gladness was upset about something.

So that I could hear better, I directed Midnight towards the commotion. However, Midnight squealed which was a horse's way of saying "no." Eventually, I was able to coax him close enough in order to listen.

Pointing at me, the angry private said, "You mean to tell me that this here black rebel broke my Camp McDonald record for leaping the ditch as well as the bar? Show me those records." Then he snatched the papers out of Johnny Reb's hands and read the statistics.

As the parchment glided to the ground, the private reached for his Colt 1849 Pocket Revolver. Pow! Pow! Pow!

The bystanders took for cover. Master Green, Sergeant Major Hart, and Johnny Reb kissed the dirt while Midnight reared up on its hind legs. This time, I didn't have a chance to grab Midnight by the neck and slide off safely to the ground. My head thumped against the red Georgia clay—lights out.

Chapter 10

WHEN I DRIFTED back into consciousness, a youthful female voice said, "Isaac, Isaac . . . Issac, you alright, sugar?"

Several minutes passed before her face came into focus; everything was a blur. Then my eyes gazed upon Miss Celia, one of Mr. Robert Mable's twelve slaves. She said, "Why aren't you in Oxford protecting Rosa Lee and Annabel like Thacker is protecting us? Have you lost your mind going off to war with Mr. Green? This is a rich man's war."

I tried to speak; however, my mouth would not move, and I wondered if I were spoiled for life.

She continued, "Sit up, sugar. Let me get you some water."

When she exited the room, I realized that I was in the sitting room of Miss Celia's six-room central hallway slave house. As I gained my bearing, I remembered that there was a front porch; and once you entered the front door, a long hallway divided both sides of her home. Two bedrooms were on each side. In the last room on the right was a table and cupboard; and directly across was the sitting room where I lounged on a long blue sofa.

As she walked back into the room, I said, "I wish we had a big house like yours, Miss Celia."

Passing me a glass of water, she said, "Thacker wishes that he had his own two room shotgun house like yours in Peaville. In three years, four slaves built the 2-story Mable House. While the slaves worked on the big house, we earned the pine wood to build this home."

"Why did it take so long?" I asked knowing that many Georgians called Oxford Peaville because peas were the primary crop.

"The men had to cut down the pine trees and cure the wood before they could hit the first nail."

After taking a few sips, I cleared my throat and asked, "Where is Master Green?"

She chuckled and said, "He is up at the big house with his cousin enjoying my southern cooking."

"How is Mrs. Almeda? Mr. Mable been married to her about . . . what? . . . seven winters now?"

"Yes sugar, everybody's doing just fine. I want to know if you have lost your mind."

"No ma'am; I was at Camp McDonald. Why am I here?"

"You've been here overnight. You fell off of that black horse. Dr. Middlebrooks at Camp McDonald told Master Green that you might have a mild concussion, and you needed to be observed overnight. They don't allow no slaves in the Camp McDonald hospital. So, Mr. Green brought you to us. I'm glad he did."

"I'm going to try and stand," I said placing the weight on my feet. Noticing that I was dressed in work pants and a cotton shirt, I was too embarrassed to ask who changed my clothes.

"Alright, hold steady," she said assisting me. In the background, I could hear the muffled voices of a few of the other slaves who lived in the home.

Pretty on the eyes, Miss Celia, who lived so far to see at least 37 winters, wore a long white ruffle dress, and her soft black hair was braided in four sections. Also, her long fingernails did not dig into my skin as I imagined. The colorful wooden bracelets on her wrist caused me to wonder if Mrs. Sally needed to accessorize the dresses that she designed for Rosa Lee. I asked, "What is that awful smell?"

"I noticed that you had a slight fever last night. Your head is cool now. That's turpentine and red onions beside the sofa. I don't reckon that your falling off the horse had anything to do with your fever. Maybe you were at the verge of catching something from some of those sickly soldiers who Master Mable talks about . . . but it ain't nothing that my home remedy can't cure."

She walked over to the edge of the sofa and showed me the contents of her turpentine concoction in a chipped blue and white delft bowl. Like a nurse, Miss Celia explained, "If Mr. Green gets a fever, you make this up for him. Cut up the onions and pour the turpentine on top, just enough to cover. In no time, he'll be just fine. Don't let him drink it. . . . He only has to smell the aroma."

"Do say? That's easy to remember. . . . What day is it?" I asked stretching my arms.

"It's the 12th instant of April. Why?"

Standing without any difficulty, I said, "The last thing I remember is breaking the record of any mounted cavalryman in the history of the Georgia Military Institute."

"We are proud of you for that, sugar."

"Thank you ma'am."

"Mr. Green said that some corned soldier started shooting up a storm because you broke his military record. Your black horse was in a terror over the gunfire and threw you up in the air. You came down hard on the ground, sugar. We praise God that it wasn't worse."

Examining my skin for any bruises, I asked, "Is Midnight alright?"

"Midnight?" she asked while sitting down in a ladder-back wooden chair with a straw seat.

"Midnight is my black horse," I said realizing that there was not a scrape on my body; however, my left arm was sore.

"Mr. Green says that the horse is fine. I think you should stay here with us until Master Mable goes back over to visit with Mrs. Almeda's family in Oxford. Then you can go back home," she said crossing her legs at the ankle.

"I have an obligation to Master Green. You don't understand."

"I understand that you almost was killed by a soldier, and you haven't step one foot in Tennessee yet."

"I'm not going to let no ornery boat-licker keep me from my dreams."

"Issac! Watch your mouth!"

"These are my dreams."

"What dreams? What do you know about this war that I don't know? Last I heard, Lincoln is emancipating the slaves. That doesn't mean that we will have new homes, sugar," she said trying to school me about the end results of the war should the Union win.

Sitting in the ladder-back wooden chair across from her, I asked, "Can you keep a secret?"

"Sure can," she said placing her right hand on her hip.

"Master Green has signed for me to get the property in Dublin, Georgia if I bring him back from the war alive."

"Really?"

"Yes ma'am."

"Well then, you get out of life as much as you put in. Let's get you fed before your ride back to Camp McDonald this morning. Did they give you all of the things you need for your horse?"

"They issued me everything but a crupper to hold my saddle in place in the steep Cumberland Mountains."

She walked down the hallway, pushed open the back screen door and yelled, "Thacker!"

Living to see at least 18 winters, Thacker entered the sitting room wearing a blue shirt and overalls. He asked, "Ma'am?"

Turning to Thacker, Miss Celia asked, "Do we have something called a crupper for a horse?"

"Yes ma'am, we have one in the stables," he said.

"What about some new riding boots? Isaac can't be wearing those worn out brown boots to Cumberland Gap," she said pointing.

"Master Mable gave those new black riding boots to me. How am I going to fight off wartime vandals if you give the boots to Isaac?" asked Thacker.

She said, "Hush up now. Master Mable says to give Mr. Green and Isaac everything they need. He will resupply us with the best."

As Thacker left the room sulking, I said, "When we go up to the big house, I'll tell Mr. Mable thank you. Miss Celia, do you know where Mr. Mable is originally from? I've learned that not all slave masters are from England."

"Now, let me think. . . . Master Mable is from a place called Scotland. He worked hard, saved his money, and bought about 450 acres of land from a man in Oxford. That's how the story goes," she said sitting back down in the chair.

"Do you know where Master Green is from? I don't know how to ask him."

"I heard Master Mable say that Mr. Green is from England. So, I think that would make him English. Why didn't you ask Annabel?"

"She don't like talking about things in the past. Besides, Mr. Mable is different from Master Green because Mr. Mable has your name and the rest of his slaves' names listed in the Mable family *Bible*. I wish Master Green would do that for us."

"I'll talk to Master Mable and see if he can convince Mr. Green to list all of your slave names in the Green family *Bible*. Let me see what I can do."

"Is Mr. Mable a planter?"

"I don't rightly know. He only has twelve slaves. Most planters have hundreds of slaves and thousands of acres of land. Some people in Mill Grove call Master Mable a planter because this is the biggest plantation around these parts. He don't act like a planter though."

"How does a planter act?" I asked sitting at the edge of the chair.

Reflecting, she said, "To the rich in this country, Mr. Green is considered a yeoman farmer. From nothing, he gained wealth by toiling and saving like Master Mable. Yeoman farmers work hand in hand with their slaves in the fields."

"I always thought that Master Green labored in the fields with my brothers because we slaves were so far behind in our work."

Smiling she said, "Not so. He works because he takes pride in his accomplishments and wants to be a part of sowing and reaping."

"You didn't answer my question."

Thinking for a moment, she said, "Some planters have so many servants and slaves that they don't have the time to have a personal relationship with them." Laughing she added, "Those planters aren't going to break a sweat in the sun either." When she saw that I was listening intently she continued, "In order to keep their lot of slaves in line, these planters likely whip and abuse their slaves. Because feeding so many is costly, they give their servants and slaves the scraps from the master's table." Hesitantly, she finally said, "Master Mable is different. To me, he is in the middle between a planter and a farmer. Regardless of what folks say, to me, he is family."

Thinking for a moment, I asked, "How do you know so much?"

"Let me ask you a few questions first."

"Alright."

"Who is the President of the United States?"

"Abraham Lincoln."

"Who is the President of the Confederate States of America?"

"Jefferson Davis."

"Who is the Governor of Georgia?"

"Umm . . . Joe Brown."

"How do you know all of these things, Isaac?"

"From being around Master Green . . ." I said in a state of confusion.

"My point exactly . . . Just like Mrs. Sally taught Annabel how to read and write, so did Master Mable's first wife, Mrs. Pheriby, taught me all of these lessons. Hence, Master Green teaches you."

"I suppose it don't matter anyhow," I said frustrated.

She stood up, leaned on the doorpost, and said, "Sugar, you are a long time dead. If it's important to you, it does matter. Those politicians are sending the young farmers to the Civil War while some of the richest influential planters are staying in the comfort of their homes. Southern mothers' hearts are torn between their sons who are fighting for the Union and their other sons who are fighting for the Confederacy. The blacks up north don't understand why men like you are parading underneath the Confederate battle flag."

I leaned my head on the back of the chair absorbing every word.

Continuing, she said "In my humble opinion, I really believe the north don't want the cotton industry to spread farther West. That's the real reason for the fight over Daniel Boone's Wilderness Trail. . . . The founders of this country spoke of independence. Sugar, we all—black and white—are entangled in freedom."

The words seemed to reverberate throughout the house.

She added, "I'm going over to the kitchen house and bring you back some breakfast."

I walked out the backdoor and headed to the slave outhouse, which was a separate building from the one at the Mable House. When I looked up, there was not a cloud above. Over twenty-one cows were grazing in a distance while three turkey vultures were flying in a circle. Many people said that vultures circling were a sign of death. However, I believed in my spirit that these birds with a long wingspan were flying to allow the wind to carry them higher into the sky. Watching them, I knew that if I had wings, I would fly away and be at rest.

On the way back to Miss Celia's house, I saw the Mable House at a great distance. There were double doors on the back of the white 2-story plantation plain house. Extended at the top of a long white pole was a black cast iron bell. Then I made a mental note to ask Miss Celia if she rang the bell for supper time or for Mrs. Mable's private school that was also on the farm.

By the front right side of the big house, Master Green was drawing water from the well. I decided to join him and find out the plans for the day.

"Well, hello there Isaac. Celia told me that you have fully recovered," Master Green said dressed in his rebel grey soldier uniform.

"How did I get here?" I asked.

"I traded in my pocket watch for the hospital's two-wheeled ambulance wagon to bring us to Robert's. When I enlisted, I didn't stop to think that you would not be able to go to the military hospital if something happened. I'm glad we were only nine miles away," he said with a sincere look.

"You loved that watch. Are you mad at me for getting thrown from Midnight?"

"No, you passed the mounted cavalry test. I tried to warn Sergeant Major Hart that you were the best rider in Georgia. In a few days, we will travel from Atlanta to Knoxville by train. A few men told me that I needed to lessen my personal load anyhow for the long march from Knoxville to Cumberland Gap."

"Will I have to ride in the stock car with the horses?"

He winked and said, "If I get my way, you will be riding in the section with me. A man's property should be beside him at all times."

I shrugged my shoulders and said, "Master Green, I thought that everyone in America who wasn't African was a native of England. Now I find out that people in the Deep South are from all parts of the world. Mr. Mable is from Scotland. Miss Celia says that you are from England."

"Yes, I came here with my father and was at one time a voluntary indentured servant."

"So you were sold on the town square like Redhead Wilson?"

"No, I looked for work and found a job as a house servant. That is why I understand to some degree what it feels like to be at the beacon call of others. You hang in there with me Isaac, and your years of servitude are over."

"I thought I was going to see more slaves at Camp McDonald."

"I suspect that when we get to Cumberland Gap, you will see black freedman and slaves. Robert tells me that Colonel Nathan Bedford Forrest has taken 45 slaves to war with him."

"Forty-five? That's the size of a company in a regiment. Is Colonel Forrest Union or Confederate?"

"Confederate," he said pouring water into two tin cups.

I said, "If Harper's Weekly is right about slavery, you would think that 45 slaves could overpower Colonel Forrest and go to the Union lines to fight against the Confederacy."

Passing me a tin cup of water that was sitting on the ledge of the well, he said, "Those 45 black slaves are smart. They know that if they fight and bring home Colonel Forrest, that they will have houses, land, and crops which can bring about wealth."

I laughed and asked, "Are you saying that I'm smart?"

Chuckling he said, "My boy, you are smart as a steel trap. Go get your things. Thacker is taking us back to Camp McDonald this morning in Robert's horse drawn carriage."

"Will I be able to say hello to Mr. Mable?"

"Robert is asleep so we better not disturb him."

As I walked back to Miss Celia's house, I noticed that she needed help carrying the food. Minutes later, I was sitting in the room with the table and cupboard as I savored every bite of the pork chops with gravy and grits.

Miss Celia said, "Slow down Isaac and chew your food. You eat like they ain't feeding you at Camp McDonald."

"They ain't feeding us like this. Besides, Master Green has a temper, and I don't want to make him late."

"Well, Thacker is gathering up the crupper and boots. Mr. Green will wait for those things if he wants you to bring him back alive."

Without notice, Thacker ran into the slave house and yelled, "Isaac! Isaac! Isaac! Hurray, the post boy delivered a message to Master Mable. The letter said that Mr. Kendrick from Big Shanty summons Master Mable to Marietta because someone just stole *The General*."

"The Union kidnapped Brigadier General Stevenson, the commander over the 42nd Regiment?" I asked ready to saddle the first horse in sight.

"No, not that General . . . the train called *The General*."

"Who is Mr. Kendrick?"

"Mr. Lemrick Kendrick is the Marietta postmaster and the richest man in Big Shanty. So, Master Mable is heading over to Marietta now. He wants me to take you and Mr. Green on over to Camp McDonald to see what Mr. Green can find out."

"Why can't Mr. Kendrick just send word back and forth by his post boy?"

"The military will trust Mr. Green with the details because he is enlisted in the Confederate States Army, not Mr. Kendrick or his post boy. Once I receive word from Mr. Green, I'll deliver the message to Master Mable because there is no telegraph service at Camp McDonald."

Miss Celia plopped down on a chair and cried out, "Oh Lordy, Billy Yank done stole *The General!*"

"Who is Billy Yank?" I asked.

She said, "Billy Yank is what they call Union soldiers. Johnny Reb is what they call Confederate soldiers."

"Do Say?" I thought that I was original when I made up the name Johnny Reb for Jonathan Russell. Then I asked, "How do you know that the Union stole the train?"

Miss Celia said, "Who else would dare steal a train in front of a Confederate training camp. Where is some parchment? You mark my words. This is the doing of Billy Yank."

Pulling me out of the house by the arm, Thacker said, "Come quickly; we can talk about this on the way to Camp McDonald."

Chapter 11

RELAXING IN THE back of the white open horse drawn carriage, Master Green stared off into the distance. The double dickey-seat provided ample room for me and Thacker, who really knew the back roads towards Camp McDonald. The afternoon sun was beaming, and everything appeared normal at the military training site.

Master Green said, "Thacker, pull over by that buck-private over there. I'm going to find out what's going on. You and Isaac stay put."

With a pike on his right shoulder, a young 42nd Regiment private was guarding Camp McDonald while bystanders on the other side of the railroad tracks gathered in front of the Lacy Hotel. Postmaster Kendrick wasn't the only one trying to find out details about the stolen locomotive. As I looked down the railroad tracks in the direction of Chattanooga, there was not a soul in sight.

"I'm Sergeant Major Abraham Green. I've been summoned to obtain details about *The General*," he said pointing towards the train depot.

The private said, "I've been given strict instructions that the Western and Atlantic Railroad is a civilian affair, and Camp McDonald is not to engage."

I said to Thacker, "Hold on to your seat."

"You mean to tell me that the very train which transports Confederate soldiers is not a concern of the Confederate

States Army? That is preposterous. I want to speak to Brigadier General Stevenson immediately. The dignitaries of Cobb County want facts now about who stole the train," said Master Green slamming his fist into his left hand.

"Sir, there is nothing I can do. Like I said, the Western and Atlantic Railroad is state-owned and is not under the jurisdiction of the Confederate States Army. Rest assured; the conductor of the train took off on foot after the train."

I admired the private, who must have lived to see at least sixteen winters, for being so calm while Master Green stood there toe to toe waving his hands in the private's face.

"How in the world can a man run and catch a moving train? What will it take for the Confederate States Army to realize that this may be the workings of the Union? I'm not Brigadier General Stevenson; however, I would take a closer look at the potential of a military coup," said Master Green having a conniption fit.

The private asked, "A military coup?"

"Son, are you deaf? If I were one of those distinguished graduates from West Point, I would issue an order for all of the bridges to be burned, telegraph wires cut and railroad ties pulled from here to Chattanooga. I've mulled this over all the way from Mill Grove to Big Shanty."

By this time, Sergeant Major Hart approached huffing and puffing. Holding his chest, he said, "Sergeant Major Green, I received word that you were back. This is a civilian matter. I would not worry because a few hours ago Mr. Kendrick took off on a horse towards Marietta in order to send a telegraph to Atlanta stating that someone stole *The General.*"

Master Green said, "That's my point. Postmaster Kendrick summoned me to obtain as many details as I can about this outlandish theft."

Horse hooves startled me, and my mouth dropped wide open when the mail carrier stopped short of Mr. Mable's carriage. I turned to Thacker and asked, "Why didn't you tell me that the post boy was a slave?"

Thacker said, "You didn't ask. You all don't have a slave post boy in Oxford?"

"No," I said trying not to stare.

Putting his elbow on his thigh and his palm under his chin, Thacker said, "Master Mable says that slaves have been delivering the United States mail in the south since the turn of the century. The rich plantation owners trust the slave with more valuable things than what's delivered in the mail."

"Do say? I have barely been out of Oxford a month, and I learn something new every day."

Still mounted on his horse, the post boy said to Sergeant Major Hart, "Mr. Kendrick says that *The Pennsylvania* is on its way here to Camp McDonald, so get ready to load up some soldiers to go after the wild train."

I said to Thacker, "It's going to take someone a long time to get here from Pennsylvania."

"No, *The Pennsylvania* is a train that stops through Marietta. Looks like Mr. Kendrick pulled some strings," Thacker said scratching his head.

Huddled in a circle, the military officers discussed which military company of the more than 2,000 soldiers at Camp McDonald would pursue *The General*."

Within a short period of time, another horse foamed in sweat rushed up from a high speed gallop. Mr. Kendrick dismounted and joined the Camp McDonald military officers as if he were the biggest toad in the puddle.

The townsfolk from across the railroad tracks migrated over in front of Camp McDonald to hear the news. When the Confederate Officers and Mr. Kendrick dispersed, Sergeant Major Hart announced, "It's all over. Conductor William Fuller has *The General*. In Ringgold, our Georgia 52nd has joined the chase on foot to catch those carpet soldiers. We should call this the Great Locomotive Chase!"

The crowd cheered, and the post boy said, "Those Yanks must have been drinking to much pot liquor to think they can steal our wild train."

As laughter filled the air, I waved goodbye to Thacker while rejoining Master Green.

Thacker yelled, "Long may your chimney smoke!"

Hightailing to catch up with Master Green and me, Sergeant Major Hart asked, "Where are you going?"

Master Green said, "I'm going to check on my horses. Why?"

"That black horse of yours has been released from duty."

Stopping in his tracks, Master Green asked, "Released from duty?"

"Private Green passed the test with flying colors and will be attached to the 2nd Brigade Light Cavalry. However, the horse is not fit for battle. The noise and commotion on the battlefield will be magnified."

"What in tarnation are you saying?"

"I'm saying don't go getting mad as a March hare."

Running towards the stables, Sergeant Major Hart yelled, "Sergeant Major Green, wait a second! Stop! Stop!"

Sweating profusely, Master Green couldn't find Midnight amongst the other horses.

Sergeant Major Hart said, "We put your horse down. He's dead."

Lunging forward, Master Green said, "I want to know who is going to pay me for my horse." With a powerful punch, Master Green slugged Sergeant Major Hart who staggered backward in a stupor. However, Sergeant Major Hart bounced back fast with fists clenched.

Rushing to the aid of Sergeant Major Hart, I put my hands on the chest of each man to hold them back from a brawl.

Wiping the blood from the corner of his mouth with his military sleeve, Sergeant Major Hart said, "I'm going to pretend that your assaulting me didn't happen."

"Isaac, let me go!" Master Green exclaimed as I grabbed him by the waist while his punches hit thin air.

"Thanks Sergeant Major Hart for understanding. That horse was like family to us," I said with a polite nod really wanting to tell Master Green "I told you so."

As Sergeant Major Hart headed towards the officer's quarters, I released Master Green. Brushing his clothes off as if he fell onto the Georgia red clay, Master Green paced back and forth in the stables. Not a word exchanged between us as he punched his right fist in the palm of his left hand.

Without notice, Johnny Reb entered and showcased a healthy Tennessee Walker horse with a shiny black coat. He said, "Sergeant Major Green, this is Chap Isaac's military issued horse named Candlelight."

Master Green stopped pacing and examined every inch of the horse.

Johnny Reb said, "Watch this."

Master Green folded his arms as he watched the horse obey Johnny Reb's verbal commands. When the horse lied down and stayed there as instructed, Master Green said, "I'll be. Will Sunlight be trained like this fine creature?"

In the distance, I heard a drummer. The rhythm of the beat was familiar.

Johnny Reb said, "A soldier in the mounted cavalry has already started working with your white horse."

The drum sound was mesmerizing, and I wanted to locate the source of the vibration.

Master Green asked, "Will Sunlight be trained before we leave for Cumberland Gap?"

Johnny Reb said, "Yes, whoever trained Sunlight before he arrived here did a fine job."

"Since Sunlight was born about five winters ago, Isaac and his brothers trained him," said Master Green with pride as he placed his left foot on an upside down wooden pail.

Leading Candlelight out of the stables, Johnny Reb turned to me and asked, "Why don't you give her a try?"

I asked, "Do you hear that drumbeat? I didn't hear drums when we arrived here."

"We have us a young drummer boy. He's too young to be enlisted; but when our 42nd captain heard those beats, the officers voted to let the boy stay with us."

Impressed, Master Green said, "He sure can play a drum."

Establishing eye to eye contact with Master Green, Johnny Reb added, "The drummer has one or the most important roles in a regiment."

"Do say? I thought the drummer's role was to make sure the soldiers marched in step. That doesn't sound like a critical job to me," I said patting my foot to the rhythm.

Johnny Reb said, "Not so. The drummer also beats out regimental commands and is the lifeline of the regiment's communications system. As an example, the drummer is the runner between outposts. In battle, getting a military command to the right post is a matter of life or death."

Master Green said, "The officers need someone trustworthy for that military position, someone who will not walk away and quit."

Johnny Reb said, "Exactly . . . Though the drummer is seen near the highest ranking officer on the battlefield, the drummer is entrusted to the office of the regimental Chaplain."

"Do say? That will be me." I wondered why Johnny Reb sounded like he was selling Master Green on the regiment having a drummer boy.

Johnny Reb continued, "This young boy said he missed his master and brother. He wants to go to Cumberland Gap."

"What are you saying?" asked Master Green.

"I'm saying that this talented boy has lifted the spirits of the troops. He is well behaved and within a day has established comradely with the 42nd."

Master Green asked, "Where did the boy come from?"

Smiling, Johnny Reb said, "He said that he came from a town called Peaville."

At a brisk pace, Master Green and I followed the sound of the drumbeat towards the right at the camp parade ground.

Dressed in an oversized military Confederate uniform, Jeremiah was drilling in line with the 42nd Regiment Georgia Volunteers Company E. As I motioned to snatch Jeremiah from formation, Johnny Reb pulled me by the arm and said, "Hold on Chap Isaac. Don't you see the pride in Sergeant Major Green's face? You have got to learn how to read all of the signs before responding." Patting me on the back, he added, "Things are going to be just fine."

Cumberland Gap, Tennessee

(March 1862-September 1862)

Chapter 12

"ALL ABOARD! SOLDIERS to the front, slaves to the back, camp is now over. Camp is now over. Soldiers to the front, slaves to the back, camp is now over. Camp is now over, all aboard," said the train conductor directing the passengers to the various steel coach cars.

An individual from behind shoved me hard and said, "Isaac, Isaac . . . Isaac, go on. You are holding up the line."

On this 16th instant of April, the others rushed to be the first to sit by the window; however, I was one of the lucky ones and touched the glass with my index finger. Perhaps this was my way of determining if I were dreaming. The locomotive was still at the station, and I felt as if I were going to pass out from the heat in the overcrowded coach car.

Jeremiah exclaimed, "I've never been on a train before! Can you believe it? If I touch the walls, do you think I'll get a splinter? How many seats do you think are in here?"

"Shhh! Be quiet. You ask too many questions," I said.

"Sergeant Major Hart says that I'm the most important link to the 42nd because I have memorized all of the drumbeats for each military command," said Jeremiah proudly.

Sitting across the aisle from us, Sergeant Major Hart said, "You sure are Jeremiah. If anyone gives you a hard time, you show them this."

"Wow! A First Georgia Ranger Badge!" Jeremiah yelled as I slouched down in my seat and nudged him.

89

Behind us, Johnny Reb said, "Chap Isaac, I knew it. I knew it. I knew you all could read."

The noise level bubbled; and a soldier asked Master Green, "Are you a scallywag?"

Another piped in and demanded, "Answer him."

Inspecting the window, I estimated if my waist could fit through the opening; however, the train was moving too fast even if I could jump.

Turning cherry red, Master Green said, "Watch your tone, private. It's no secret. We belong to the Emory College community. It's just a stone's throw from my farm. Education is engrained in our culture."

"I know all about your culture, alright. During a college debate, those Emory students stated that Georgia should not secede. You are a James Andrews scallywag!" exclaimed the soldier who lunged forward to grab Master Green by the collar.

Johnny Reb pulled the soldier down hard upon the seat while Jeremiah polished his worn badge with his rebel grey shirttail.

"Pay them no never mind," said Sergeant Major Hart, "We can use Jeremiah to our advantage. If the enemy sees Jeremiah with papers, they will likely assume the documents are irrelevant and ignore him because they will think that slaves in Georgia can't read. All the better, I say."

When the men wouldn't calm down, I wondered if the conductor would stop the train and throw us off.

Sergeant Major Hart screamed, "Enough! Don't be a C.S.A. Sergeant killer."

Jeremiah asked, "What did I do?"

With his index finger against his right cheek, Sergeant Major Hart said, "No, not you, Jeremiah, these privates need to settle down. However, there is no way you could have known the badge was a Georgia Ranger badge unless you could read. It's unfathomable that slaves can read."

The tension in the air was thick when Jeremiah said, "But I did read it." Pointing he added, "It says right here: Georgia Range—"

Putting my hand over Jeremiah's mouth, I said, "It's just a coincidence. I'm sure he guessed what the badge said. He is just a parrot."

As Jeremiah murmured under his breath and pulled against my hand, Johnny Reb stood up and exclaimed, "Unity!"

Everyone looked baffled and quieted down.

He added, "The reason why Jeremiah and Chap Isaac are riding up here with us is because of unity. The conductor said 'Soldiers to the front.' We, Confederates, are fighting for the Southern Cause. I have a newspaper clipping here that says the Confederate States Army is estimating 13,000 deaths alone of our soldiers at Shiloh. Who wants to make it back to Newton County alive?"

Everyone, including me, raised hands high in the air.

"You will only weaken our communications line if we don't work together as one team which includes Jeremiah. Be proud of who we are collectively."

Escaping my grip, Jeremiah said, "We ain't no scallywags. I want to be like those real black soldiers with the Texas and Georgia Rangers, the ones who are going to fight at the Battle of Mur-frees-bee."

A few soldiers laughed and Sergeant Major Hart said, "That's the upcoming Battle of Murfreesborough in Tennessee. Jeremiah, let's just keep it a secret between us boys about blacks in the Confederate States Army. We wouldn't want President Jefferson Davis getting his pants in a wad. Now would we?"

"People should know. I want to be just like those black soldiers," said Jeremiah putting on his badge.

Master Green said, "How does Jeremiah know about the Battle of Murfreesborough?"

Sergeant Major Hart said, "You must remember that the drummer is closest to the commanding officer. He is privy to a great deal of information. There is word that Confederate Colonel Forrest has enlisted 65 slaves which includes 45 of his very own. Some black teamsters, cooks and even soldiers will likely be at the Battle of Murfreesborough. Just as you plan to manumit Isaac's family for their loyalty to the south, so will the Colonel be manumitting these 65 slaves."

"Do say? I thought there were only 45 slaves serving," I said surprised that Jeremiah was already entrenched in the thread of military command.

Master Green said, "When we get to Knoxville away from the troops, I'll school Jeremiah on the appropriate time to discuss military tactics."

Sergeant Major Hart turned to Jeremiah and said, "Once you stepped foot on this train, you became an official Confederate drummer. As First Sergeant Russell said this is about 'unity.' There is only one color in Company E, and it is rebel grey."

The soldiers exclaimed, "Rebel grey!"

Smiling from ear to ear, Jeremiah motioned to speak, but I pinched him hard and whispered, "Keep your mouth shut. You should have stayed back in Oxford. You talk too much."

Sergeant Major Hart continued, "Everyone listen and listen good."

Johnny Reb took out his journalist pad and quill.

"As you know, there were five men in our Company E to die of illness at Camp McDonald. Chap Issac, lead us in a moment of silence for Brewer, Biggers, Harris, Middlebrooks and Walker," said Sergeant Major Hart.

As I stood against the wall of the train, I searched the hearts of the men in the coach car and said, "Let's bow our heads."

The minute of total quiet brought about calm in an otherwise overheated situation. I said, "So mote it be."

Sergeant Major Hart continued, "Let me brief you all on what we will likely face in the Cumberland Mountains. . . ."

Jeremiah said, "I know. I know." By the time I could put my hand across his mouth, his eyes became bright. Then he said, "Isaac, Isaac, Isaac, look out the window and see all of those people walking alongside the train."

I said, "Don't try to change the subject now." When I turned to look, slaves were walking without their masters for miles.

Johnny Reb said, "Jeremiah, those are what they call contraband."

"I bet they are trying to make it to East Tennessee closer to Union lines," I said noticing a slave mother, who was wearing an off-white cotton African brocade dress trimmed in teal, with a baby on her back in a large colorful brown and teal scarf baby carrier. This caused me to pause and pray for Rosa Lee and Jacob. If the 42nd wasn't successful at Cumberland Gap, where would our Green family go?

Sergeant Major Hart was likewise distracted by the refugees.

Master Green said to everyone in the coach car, "As Sergeant Major Hart was saying, we need to understand the political landscape of Cumberland Gap, which is the trail that was first recorded by a Dr. Thomas Walker. The Union 3rd and 4th Tennessee Regiments were originally formed by a man from Tennessee himself, Samuel Carter. You see that slave contraband outside the window?"

As heads nodded, Sergeant Major Hart chimed in, "The Union 3rd and 4th Tennessee Regiments were formed with refugees from East Tennessee."

Jeremiah asked, "Are they slaves too?"

Sergeant Major Hart said, "No, our very own Colonel Rains reports that when Cumberland Gap came under our control, the mountaineers became refugees. Now these same Union conscripts will be angry for revenge upon our Confederate Regiments once we arrive. Understood?"

"Yes sir!" exclaimed the soldiers.

Sergeant Major Hart said, "Our job is to make sure that the new Major General Morgan doesn't take control of Cumberland Gap."

Johnny Reb said, "I thought Morgan was Confederate."

"Men, I need your undivided attention." As the men settled down from talking about the contraband, Sergeant Major Hart added, "Major General W. Morgan is Union. Colonel John Hunt Morgan is Confederate and commands the Army of Tennessee Cavalry Brigade."

A soldier piped in and asked, "How are we going to know the Union versus the Confederates in Tennessee?"

Jeremiah turned around intently to listen because his role depended on knowing the difference.

Sergeant Major Hart passed around a picture of Major General Morgan and said, "The Union Morgan has organized the 7th Division of the Army of Ohio with the 3rd and 4th Tennessee Regiments attached."

Jeremiah said, "We are with the Confederate Forces Department of East Tennessee. Our 2nd Brigade includes Tennessee, Alabama, Georgia, North Carolina and Virginia."

"That's right, Jeremiah. You are a quick study," said Master Green.

"Like Jeremiah said, in our Confederate 2nd Brigade is the 4th Tennessee Infantry Regiment under the leadership of Colonel McMurry. On the other hand, the Union 4th Tennessee Infantry Regiment is under the command of Colonel Robert Johnson, the son of U.S. Senator Andrew Johnson from Greeneville, Tennessee."

Throwing his quill in the air, Johnny Reb said, "I can't keep all of these names straight. All I want to do is fight some Yanks; you lead the way Sergeant Major!"

The soldiers cheered. However, by the look on Sergeant Major Hart's face, I wondered if he was concerned that we could easily be lead into enemy territory. I whispered, "What's wrong Sergeant Major Hart?"

He said, "U.S. Senator Andrew Johnson was the only southern senator not to quit his post when the south seceded, plus he has the backing of President Abraham Lincoln. I have a gut feeling that U.S. Senator Andrew Johnson's son and Unionist Robert Johnson will receive a wealth of resources at Cumberland Gap."

"Do say? Do you think Brigadier General Stevenson knows Colonel Robert Johnson?"

Sergeant Hart asked, "Why would you ask that?"

"Master Green says that you can count for days all of the Union and Confederate Generals who are graduates from West Point. Master Green says Confederate Major General Kirby Smith graduated from West Point. What about this Major General Morgan who we will be fighting against at Cumberland Gap?"

Sergeant Major Hart thought for a moment and said, "As a matter of fact, Major General W. Morgan with the Union did graduate from West Pont. I've heard people talk about it, but never gave it this much thought. Maybe that's what townsfolk really mean when they say that brother is fighting against brother in this Civil War. Perhaps the war is more about fraternal brothers. What's your point?"

"If all of our Confederate Generals know the Union Major General Morgan, maybe there might not be much action at Cumberland Gap. I'm just saying."

The concern look on Sergeant Major Hart's face remained, and he looked out of the window at the Georgia forest.

As the trained rolled towards Chattanooga with our final destination of Knoxville, Johnny Reb pulled out a newspaper clipping and said, "From here to Ringgold, let's identify all of the stops during the locomotive chase of *The General.*"

Jeremiah asked, "Which General, Union or Confederate?"

The coach car filled with laughter; then Johnny Reb broke out into a song called "Goober Peas." Unfortunately, there was not a peanut to be found.

Chapter 13

ON THE 29TH instant of April, our 42nd Regiment was not 24 hours settled before the shots sounded throughout the Cumberland Mountains. My ears were ringing because of the Union cannon and gunfire. Looking up from the base of Cumberland Gap, I surveyed the location of the enemy.

A few feet away, Colonel R. J. Henderson signalled for Jeremiah to drum the *Long Roll.* As the Confederate Forces 2nd Brigade marched into battle, the attached Tennessee Rhett Artillery rolled our cannon, that we affectionately named Long Tom, into position. This was my visual cue to travel up the reverse slope of Cumberland Gap and scout out the exact location of the Union 4th Tennessee Infantry Regiment. Within minutes, my military issued gaited mule trotted steady around the four mile incline while Confederates on picket duty pointed the way.

There were locations where the slopes were so steep that the mule almost lost footing, and the rocks tumbled to the surface below. Hearing the nearby Cumberland River, my dry mouth longed for a refreshing drink.

I remembered being told that over 87 summers ago Daniel Boone, a great pioneer, forged the trail that made these mountains, river, and gap an original gateway to the West. On this day, the Union was fighting to take control of this critical track of land.

Boom! Boom! Boom! As my heart pounded against my chest cavity, the Union 4th Tennessee Infantry Regiment soldiers fired down upon the valley from the Pinnacle. The smell of gun powder filled the air.

There was a great explosive sound that pierced the air up to the Pinnacle, and a Union soldier screamed, "I've been hit!" Boom! Boom! Boom!

A Union officer yelled, "Cease fire! We are out of food and supplies. Cease fire! Load the injured up on the wagon and take them to the fort hospital. How many are there?"

Boom! Boom! Boom! The injured soldier paused and said, "Fifteen, at least."

When I turned to the left, the Union hospital wagon travelled towards me. Time was of the essence for me to abandon my position and alert Colonel Henderson. Knowing that the enemy would take the narrow path from whence I came, my only option was to travel down a roadway that was far less travelled.

Blowing against my face, the wind was brisk, and the tree limbs from the narrow trail whipped against my body. I dared not scream. With my right hand, I pulled out my light cavalry saber and did my best to cut the tall brush away. Then I tasted blood, but could not identify the source of the wound.

Once I was back at the base of the mountain, Jeremiah asked, "You look bad. You okay?"

"Yes," I said catching my breath.

"Did we get them?" he asked with bright eyes.

"Fifteen or so . . . Tell Colonel Henderson that the Union ordered a cease fire," I said looking at the rips on the sleeves of my cavalryman uniform. The mule didn't fare well either during the descent of the mountain.

Suddenly the silence became deafening after Jeremiah's *Cease Fire* drumbeat. Walking the gaited mule back the rest of the way to the camp, I saw three bloody Confederate privates on stretchers.

Holding his journalist pad, Johnny Reb said, "The Union wounded one of ours from the North Carolina Infantry Regiment and two from the 3rd Georgia Infantry Battalion. Help me take them up to Cave Gap."

I asked, "Lieutenant Colonel Stovall's 3rd?"

"Yes, now help me get our boys up to Cave Gap."

"If we go up the forward slope now, the Union will retaliate for sure," I said checking my head. There was blood on my hands.

"Our doctors have turned Cave Gap into a makeshift hospital away from the line of fire. We need a hand, Chap," he said placing his writing pad in his pocket and picking up one end of a stretcher.

The soldiers were moaning, so I hurried to tie up the mule.

Sergeant Major Hart said, "Good job, Private Green. When we go up to Cave Gap, have the nurse examine those whip marks on your arm and the cut on your face."

Master Green came running towards me and said, "Where in tarnation is that Billy Yank? I'm going to kill him myself for laying a hand on you, Isaac. By the size of that lash, I'd say they used a chicotte whip."

I said, "They—"

Cherry red, Master Green added, "I told you that those Yankees don't care nothing for the slave. This is proof. Look how they put all of those bruises on your face," he said examining every inch of my body.

"But—"

"But nothing . . ." Mounting Sunlight, he said, "At what location on the reverse slope did they catch you? I don't need Long Tom. I'll kill them bare-handedly myself."

"Hold on!" I exclaimed.

"Hold on nothing . . . How did you get away?"

"Hold on, I say. The mountain elements did all of this to my skin. I had to recut a trail down the rugged terrain or I would have been captured."

Saddled on Sunlight, he asked, "Billy Yank didn't whip you?"

"No sir, the Cumberland Mountain tore into me something awful."

Shaking his head, Sergeant Major Hart said, "Sergeant Major Green, why don't you come down from the horse and help us get these three soldiers to the hospital at Cave Gap?"

Trying to conceal his embarrassment, Master Green took the other end of the stretcher with Johnny Reb. Two more privates joined us, and we transported the injured up the steep hill into the mouth of the cave.

Upon entry, amazement overwhelmed me when there were more men dying from diseases than war injuries. Each of the three wounded were removed from a stretcher and placed on individual hospital straw mattresses. Then we leaned every stretcher against the exterior wall of the cave.

Johnny Reb said, "Chap Isaac, come follow me. I have something to show you."

Back inside not far past the makeshift hospital, there was the name "Rains" inscribed on the left side of the cave wall. I asked, "Who is Rains?"

"Confederate Colonel Rains was commander of our 2nd Brigade before we arrived at Cumberland Gap. As you know, now we are under the command of Brigadier General Stevenson."

"How did Colonel Rains write his name on the cave wall?" I asked noticing that his signature was in climbing distance.

"I was told that he used soot from a candle. Come on. I want to show you King Solomon's Temple," he said a few paces away.

"I'm not going any further than this. I will have to crawl on my hands and knees to get through this cave. Even Colonel Rains was smart enough to use a candle to see in the pitch black."

"Stop exaggerating. You may have to squat a little."

"Tell me one reason why I should care about this cave?"

"Alright, you should care because of Cudjo."

"Who? I don't know no Cudjo."

"Cudjo, the runaway slave." Sounding theatrical, Johnny Reb said, "The legend goes that there was a runaway slave boy named Cudjo. When he saw our boys in grey coming, Cudjo ran deep inside Cave Gap." There was an echo as Johnny Reb spoke. "The story goes that our men attacked Cudjo before he could make it to Union lines in Kentucky. Do you think it's true?"

"Do I look like the slave expert to you?"

"Tell me what you would have done if you saw a team of angry Confederates coming."

I thought for a minute and said, "The tale is hogwash. Kentucky, Tennessee, and Virginia state lines all met right here at Cumberland Gap. I smelt the stink on those East Tennessee Union soldiers up at the Pinnacle. That's how close I was to them."

"I'm listening," he said taking out his writing pad and quill. I wondered if the light from the distant sun was bright enough in the cave for him to scribble his notes.

I continued, "Cumberland Gap is swarming with East Tennessee Yankees. Moments ago, I could have changed sides in a split second. If I were Cudjo, I would have staked out the camp to find a soldier in blue; then I would have made a run for it. Who makes up these tales anyway?"

"So, when you were up at the top of the mountain, did you think about making a run for it?"

"Never crossed my mind," I said.

Then we heard Jeremiah drumming the *Retreat* beat.

From a distance, Sergeant Major Hart yelled, "Move out!" As I turned to exit Cave Gap, he added, "Not you, Private Green. The nurse here is going to check you over. Those cuts look real bad."

I scanned the area to see if he was talking to me. At Camp McDonald, I was not allowed to go one inch of the military hospital.

In a hard-nosed southern tone, Nurse Minnie said, "Come sit on this rock and let me take a look."

Once the clean gauze with alcohol touched my sweaty face, I jumped.

Her facial expression was grave, and she said, "Hold steady, so I don't come near your eye."

"How can you stay in here? The smell is awful," I said as the field surgeon checked over the three wounded soldiers.

She said, "I've been here since January. You get use to it. There are six nurses at Cumberland Gap. We take turns bathing the sick soldiers, washing their undergarments, and passing out food when there is food to give."

Curiously, I asked, "Have you ever tended to a slave before?"

"I am a volunteer of the Ladies Soldiers' Relief Society. If a Confederate Sergeant says you are a soldier, then that's what you are to me," she said wearing a plain long white dress with a pin on apron.

"Do say?"

"To be honest, tending to a patient with war wounds is kind of exciting. We haven't seen much action here."

"My prayer is that these are the only scrapes I will have during the war."

She demanded, "Take off your shirt. I need to see how deep the cuts are."

I blushed because the only women to see my bare chest were Rosa Lee and my mother.

"Here, let me help you." She moved so fast that I groaned as she lifted my arm.

When she showed me the slashes, I asked, "What are you going to do?"

In a matter of fact tone, she said, "I'm going to clean your arm and bandage you up. Then I want you to come back in about three days, and I'll change the dressing."

This was my first time at a hospital, even if the location was a cool damp cave. My mind drifted back to the story about Cudjo. I asked, "Have you heard the story about the runaway slave?"

"Yes, I've heard the soldiers joke about him. Why?"

"Do you know why a runaway slave would escape into this cave to hide when Tennessee is pro-Union? I can't figure this out."

"Even though Tennessee, for the most part, is pro-Union doesn't mean that everyone here is against slavery. I often wonder if the fable continues as a way to incite fear against Confederates."

"Do say?"

Her left eyebrow raised, and she asked brazenly, "When you are free, are you going to be like the nurse named Harriett Tubman?"

"I've never heard of her," I said looking into Nurse Minnie's deep blue eyes.

"Word is that Harriett Tubman is helping contrabands escape to freedom."

"Do say? After the war, I will be better able to help others."

"Really?"

"Yes, I can't give the details, but there is a bright future for me."

"Well, don't you go worrying about Cudjo. We nurses, like Harriett Tubman, have a way of helping people," she said winking and revealing shiny white teeth. She added, "Are you a believer?"

"Yes," I said with conviction.

"Well, that's all that matters: God, family, and country. What country are you from?"

"The state of Georgia," I said knowing that at the Green farm one's country represented the state in which a person lived.

"You do your best and make Georgia proud. The rest will take care of itself."

At that moment, Nurse Minnie helped me to better understand that there was no clear way to look at a person and determine if they were friend or foe of the slave. One thing was for sure. Mrs. Fair from Newtown County was right. In no time, Nurse Minnie opened up to me.

Chapter 14

A FEW WEEKS after Major General Morgan's Union troops retreated from the Pinnacle to resupply, a massive hail and wind storm blew down most of the trees. I joined our Company E in chopping the wood as other soldiers in our 2nd Brigade hauled off the load from Cumberland Gap by wagon trail. Fortunately, the camp was calm near quitting time for Brigadier General Carter Stevenson's 4,500 men of infantry, cavalry, and artillery on this 31st instant of May.

Johnny Reb whispered, "Soon it will be too dark to continue. We in Company E are heading back to camp. You going with us to the watering hole tonight?"

As I pulled the damp shirt away from my skin, I said, "Leaving the camp and drinking moonshine is forbidden. I haven't left Cumberland Gap since we arrived."

"There are several of us who need to slip away from all of the sickness. We can't take much more of this waiting around for something to happen."

"You need to come to my Sunday service. I can't think of one sick man in my parish," I said wiping my brow with the arm of my shirt.

"Half of your parishioners aren't getting sick because of all the watermelon they are eating," said Johnny Reb.

"Are you serious?" I asked not understanding where the conversation was headed.

"Yes Chap, a few men are spiking the watermelon with liquor."

"Do say? How are they doing that?" I asked throwing the axe on the back of a six mule military wagon.

"They cut a hole in the watermelon, pour in the spirits and recap the plug."

"Do say?"

"Do you want some watermelon?"

"What? Tell me you aren't like those cowboys out West. Are you going to offer me rock candy and churned ice cream too?" I asked getting angry.

Sounding like a reporter, he said, "Whoa, there's nothing wrong with eating ice cream. In fact, a black freed woman named Aunt Sallie Shadd perfected the ice cream with cream, sugar, and fruit. The President of the United States, George Washington, himself enjoyed every bite."

I said, "You won't let me get mad at you. Will you?"

"Not if I can help it. Well, the men are out of spirits, and we are headed out tonight. You don't have to partake. Simply go with us to get a change of scenery."

"What watering hole is going to let a slave enter the front door?" I asked as Johnny Reb and I hopped in the back of the wagon.

"You leave the details to us. We can get you into any watering hole in East Tennessee." He pulled two Union navy shirts from his knapsack. "We are going to wear these."

"Where did you get Union shirts?" I asked.

"If I tell you, I'll have to kill you," he said as other men from Company E piled in behind us.

"Is this some kind of joke?" I asked as our heads bobbed up and down due to the rocky ride down the mountain.

"No joke at all. After we wash up and put on clean clothes, we are walking a few miles over into Middlesborough, Kentucky," said Johnny Reb trying to keep his balance.

The wagon stopped short of our white tents near Cumberland Gap village. I never witnessed a group of men change so quickly. As we exited our military dwellings, work clothing was strewn near the center pole. In total, there were nine of us walking towards Middlesborough through the back woods.

Within an hour or so, we approached a single-pen log cabin that displayed little charm. On the front porch were watermelons stacked three rows high. Once my foot was planted on the limestone step, I was amazed that the place overflowed with soldiers dressed in blue. No one inside this juke joint lived more than 30 winters, and the atmosphere was jovial.

To our right were a square table and two wooden chairs. As two soldiers also in blue stood, Johnny Reb and I quickly occupied the seats. Lanterns glowed as a cool breeze flowed through the adjacent window.

A cute server walked over to us and said in a raspy voice, "Is he your bodyguard?"

"Who? This man?" asked Johnny Reb pointing to me.

"Who do you think I'm talking about?" she asked tucking her blonde hair behind her ear.

Johnny Reb said, "He is one of those black freedmen on furlough from the Louisiana Native Guards. He doesn't speak good English. He's French."

On cue, I shifted in the seat and crossed my legs like a true gentleman.

Inspecting my Union shirt, she said, "I thought the Louisiana Native Guards were Confederate soldiers. New Orleans had a Grand Review and everything. There were about 1,300 black soldiers marching in step with over 27,000 in total."

"As it turns out, the Confederates in New Orleans wouldn't let those black freedmen fight. Imagine that." Patting me on the back, Johnny Reb added, "This man right here is proof that the Louisiana Native Guards will in no time be attached to the Union. I might be wrong, but I'd say these black men will likely make history for being the first colored troops to serve on both sides." Then he passed her a news clipping.

With a priceless facial expression, she said, "Now it all makes sense. Some people were making a fuss about an art drawing that showed black soldiers in grey. Then later another drawing showed the same black soldiers in blue. Well, I'll be. It's the same group of soldiers. Both drawings are correct."

"This news article states that the New Orleans Grand Review of the Louisiana Native Guards was just for show," said Johnny Reb standing to point out the exact line in the article.

"Well, that's a shame. Seems like if you are free, you should be able to fight with and for whomever you want," she said giving the paper back to Johnny Reb who took his seat.

She continued, "Did you see those Confederates at Cumberland Gap chopping down all of those trees today so they can see the Union better. Those Department of Tennessee Confederates sure are dumb."

"We—"

"The gentlemen from New Orleans said 'yes' in French. The entire Union Army witnessed those scoundrels clearing the forest. It sure is dumb," said Johnny Reb nudging me on the knee.

"What you having?" she asked.

"We will have two Old Grand-Dads," said Johnny Reb tapping his fingers on the table.

"No—"

"The Frenchman means that he will have water instead. I'll have the Old Grand-Dad," said Johnny Reb.

With her hands on her hip, she said, "I've got one better than that. Why don't you try the Tennessee Sour Mash Whiskey?"

Johnny Reb said, "Never heard of it."

"There is this up and coming kid name Jasper Daniel who is one of the best moonshiners in these parts. We call him Jack. Everybody is raving about his brew."

I nudged Johnny Reb and whispered in his ear.

"Pardon me; I must translate for the Frenchman. He wants to know how the boy started his business," said Johnny Reb.

"He learned from a man name Dan Call who owns a dry goods store in Lynchburg, Tennessee. Word is that Jack's uncle is serving in the Confederate States Army under Colonel Nathan Bedford Forrest, but we don't hold that against the boy," she said frowning.

Johnny Reb winked at me and said, "Why of course not. As proof, I'll have the Tennessee Sour Mash Whiskey."

After she left to obtain the drinks, I was still upset about her earlier comment and said, "We didn't chop down those trees. Those trees fell down from the wind storm. Can you believe that these people think we are some dumb Confederates? Why was she frowning about Colonel Forrest? He has Jack's uncle serving with black Confederates. That's monumental."

"I am not here to set the record straight. I just want to have my Tennessee Sour Mash Whiskey from little Jack Daniel and head back to camp before the bugle sounds *Tattoo*. You have to work with me and stick to just the French words 'oui' and 'non,'" said Johnny Reb turning to see if anyone was outside the window.

"I didn't even know I was speaking French. Who are all of these people anyway?" I asked. There was not a single chair empty in this juke joint, and many were standing on the outside waiting to gain entry.

"I think that's the good part about being in East Tennessee. Union and Confederates can easily mingle and no one knows the difference. Did you hear about the North Carolina and 3rd Georgia Battalion deserters?"

"All I know is that after the three soldiers were wounded, a few of their comrades took off like a bat out of Cave Gap. Have they been caught?"

"I think so. Did you hear about a few of our soldiers on picket duty who shot a hole in their hands just to get approved for sick furlough?"

"I don't see why. Mean Stevenson isn't allowing anybody to go home."

"Is that what they call Brigadier General Stevenson?"

Before I could respond, a man wearing khaki overalls sat on a stool and began to play the banjo. The tune was catchy as the musician sang:

> *"Lay down, boys, gonna take a little nap,*
> *Lay down, boys, gonna take a little nap,*
> *Lay down, boys, gonna take a little nap—*
> *fourteen miles to the Cumberland Gap.*
>
> *Come on, boys, no time to nap,*
> *Come on, boys, no time to nap,*
> *Come on, boys, no time to nap—*
> *We're gonna raise Cain on the Cumberland Gap."*

With heaven as my witness, I don't know where all of the women came from when the area near the bar filled with people dancing and soldiers screaming like cowboys. My foot was tapping to the beat; and at that moment, I felt freedom.

The server returned with our drinks and said, "Here you go."

Johnny Reb asked, "How much do I owe you?"

"Nothing, that officer over there picked up your tab."

When I looked across the room, the 42nd Colonel R. J. Henderson tipped his hat towards Johnny Reb and me. Beside him were the 3rd Georgia Infantry Battalion Lieutenant Colonel Marcellus Stovall and their boss, 2nd Brigadier General Stevenson. I asked, "Who is that man on the other side of Stevenson?"

Johnny Reb said, "You have got to be kidding me. That's Major General Kirby Smith. He's the big wig over us all."

With my elbows on the table and the palms of my hands on my forehead, I knew we were doomed.

Within seconds, an influx of soldiers swarmed the juke joint, and the banjo music stopped as everyone inside scrambled. However, there was only one front door.

I screamed over the noise from the chairs scrapping the floor and feet trampling, "Who are these Confederate soldiers!"

Johnny Reb stood and exclaimed, "They are the Confederate military police that President Jeff Davis formulated to identify national spies!"

"We aren't spies."

He plucked his shirt and said, "With these blue uniforms on, we look like spies."

"Now what are we going to do?" I asked as Johnny Reb and I made a dash through the open window.

To my surprise, there was a black slave with his hand extended helping us to escape. He pointed to a wagon near the back of the juke joint and Johnny Reb and I hopped onto our getaway ride.

I asked, "What just happened?"

Johnny Reb asked, "Do you know this man?" Somehow there were only the three of us as the slave drove the horses through the mountain range back towards Cumberland Gap.

As my heart pounding against my chest cavity, I was able to get a glimpse of the miraculous view of the Cumberland Mountains as the moonlit sky dazzled the green earth. Crickets and frogs demanded to be heard while deer dashed in and out of the forest. Taking a deep breath, I could not fathom where this journey would lead us.

Johnny Reb said, "I didn't even get a chance to taste that Tennessee whiskey by little Jack Daniel."

"You ought to be glad because your breath would reek of sin," I said waiting for the bolt of lightning to fall from the sky. I added, "Do you know what they do to soldiers who leave the camp without permission?"

"Who are you asking? This is my first time out of the state of Georgia," he said with his right eyebrow raised.

The ride back felt like eternity. As the wagon pulled up to the sea of tents, the bugle sounded *Tattoo*. There were only five minutes to spare before bed check.

The slave rushed us along to our tent. When we arrived inside, Johnny Reb and I were the only ones who made it back in time. Extending his hand, he said, "I'm Josiah. Colonel Henderson asked my Master Stovall for help in getting you boys back safely to camp. Colonel Henderson said that he made a promise to a Mrs. Fair that he was obliged to keep. A wrath will fall upon the camp tomorrow."

Miffed, Johnny Reb asked, "Who is Mrs. Fair?"

I said, "She is like a Fairy Godmother to me back in Newton County."

"Why thank you, Josiah. Who are you?" asked Johnny Reb.

"I'm the bodyguard and forager for Lieutenant Colonel Stovall. Two of Master Stovall's men from the 3rd Georgia Infantry Battalion were wounded in that attack a few days back. I guess you heard about the others under his command who tried to leave the army as a result."

"Yes, we heard. What do I owe you for delivering us to safety?" asked Johnny Reb.

Josiah said, "You don't owe me nothing. Isaac here is a small town hero to our slave community. We slaves aim to make sure he continues to fight beside you, First Sergeant Russell. You are a hero in your own right for allowing Isaac to be treated like a man."

We heard loud noises of men settling in for the evening.

Opening up the flap of the tent, Josiah turned to us and said, "You young boys both listen and here me good. If you ever get in a world of hurt, you pray my prayer of faith out loud so that God can hear you." He took our hands, bowed his head, and said, "Oh Lord, my God, is there no help for the widow's son? Amen." In a flash Josiah was gone, just like an angel swooping down from a heavenly chariot to bring us back home.

Chapter 15

THE NEXT MORNING, Jeremiah drummed the *1ˢᵗ Sergeant Call.* Unexpectedly, Johnny Reb and I were summoned to the Olde Mill Inn which was converted into a temporary Confederate Headquarters at Cumberland Gap. The building was a rectangular pen log house with a large water wheel, which before the war worked in conjunction with a triangular stone iron furnace for the production of precious metal for neighboring manufacturing companies.

The temperature inside the Olde Mill Inn was hot upon entry through the front door. The officers of the 2ⁿᵈ Brigade were gathered around the Gillows of Lancaster 12-seater table. Brigadier General Stevenson said, "Everyone have a seat."

As Johnny Reb sat down, I stood against the wall with the bookcases.

"Private Green, you take a seat beside First Sergeant Russell."

After I sat down, Josiah, Lieutenant Colonel Stovall's bodyguard, came from the kitchen with a pitcher of water on a silver tray. On this 1ˢᵗ instant of June, he wore a white shirt, black vest and pants. As he tilted the pitcher towards the crystal stemware, Josiah whispered in my ear, "Remember my prayer of faith."

I whispered, "Oh yes, I remember the widow's son rising from the dead at the gate of Nain."

"Never stop searching for truth," Josiah said as he filled Johnny Reb's glass.

"Gentlemen, today is the day of reckoning. There are soldiers at this camp who are breaking the rules set by the Confederate States Army. We have reached the boiling point where there will be no Grand Review for the traitors of the Confederate Forces Department of Tennessee," said Brigadier General Stevenson, who was at the head of the table.

Johnny Reb wiped his brow and took a sip of water. His knee was shaking while a ring of sweat emerged from under his armpit.

"These traitors slip off the campgrounds and pilferage from the mouths of East Tennessee mothers and children at the expense of our fine reputation. These men spread lies that the Confederate States Army is stripping the tin roofs off of the homes of southern families to fund our military operations. These same spies provide the enemy with vital information about our supply lines here at Cumberland Gap."

I jumped when Brigadier General Stevenson slammed his fist down on the table.

"Not only that, these despicable soldiers display their drunken stupor for the locals to witness," he said gazing for guilt within my eyes.

There was a long pause. Then he said, "You two, tell me one good reason why I shouldn't put you both in front of the firing squad." His eyes continued to pierce through my soul. As a slave, I dared not respond.

Johnny Reb said, "Leadership."

"How is sneaking out of the camp to go to that House of Jezebel leadership?" asked Brigadier General Stevenson with his left eyebrow raised.

"Sir, you were called to be a correspondent for the Atlanta Southern Confederacy newspaper. I am an aspiring journalist. Documenting the total experience of the war so that people will be able to one day read the Confederate side of the story, I believe is an admirable feat. You, sir, are indeed a role model," Johnny Reb said with conviction. I was even moved.

Brigadier General Stevenson's jaw relaxed; and he said, "Well then, in a few hours you will lead the infantry, and Private Green will lead the cavalry out in a military procession for the punishment of the deserters from the North Carolina Infantry Regiment."

Instinctively, Johnny Reb stood and said, "Sir, you can't have Chaplain Isaac lead the cavalry in a procession which results in the punishment of white soldiers. You will incite anger in the hearts of the men."

As I leaned forward to get a better visual of the other officers' expressions, Brigadier General Stevenson asked, "Does Private Green leading the cavalry in a military procession incite you?"

I leaned back to better hear Johnny Reb's response. After all, this was a man in whom I grew to entrust my military existence. He said, "I would be proud to see any man, including Chaplain Isaac, have the honor to lead the 2nd Brigade in a procession."

42nd Colonel Henderson chimed in and asked, "Why should the other men see Private Green any differently than you?"

Sitting down, Johnny Reb said, "You don't get it. These soldiers' friends were wounded a few weeks ago; one comrade even lost an arm. Worst case, these deserters were expecting to die at the feet of the Union, not bruised by the hands of their own Confederate States Army. These despicable soldiers, as you call them, will see Chaplain Isaac's leading the cavalry as a slap in the face for the Southern Cause. You do not need dissension amongst the ranks, sir."

"Enough!" exclaimed Brigadier General Stevenson, "This is not up for discussion." He stood, turned to 42nd Colonel

Henderson, and said, "Tell your drummer boy to prepare the troops."

All of the officers stood, and I was escorted out of the building to join the 14th Battalion Tennessee Cavalry in the procession. For the first time at Cumberland Gap, I held my shoulders back and my head up high. In the distance, I heard Jeremiah's drumbeats. Prearranged, a Tennessee cavalryman approached me with Candlelight. To say the air was somber was an understatement. As the cavalry officer walked me through the formation, Johnny Reb took instructions from the infantry officers.

The entire processional comprised over 3,000 soldiers. As Jeremiah drummed *Slow March* in line with 180 drummers, Johnny Reb led the infantry into a square "U" formation several rows deep while surrounding the deserters. Then I looked for Master Green; however, he was not easily located.

Once the infantry was in position, Lieutenant Colonel James Carter and I led over 400 cavalrymen in closing the fourth side of the square formation. The sound of hooves trotting weighed down the spirits of the troops. However, the sea of cavalrymen's yellow trimmed caps and jackets gave me the feeling that I was finally attached to something larger than life. Then Jeremiah led the drummers in *Hail to the Chief*, and Major General Kirby Smith entered onto the parade ground.

Shortly afterwards, the six deserters were stripped of all military ranks and tied to a stake of arms in order to be whipped with cowhide against their bare backs. Because the setting was grave, only I was aware of the tears which filled Jeremiah's eyes.

A deserter sobbed, "Why are you torturing me while my father's slaves remain under his care back home? He loves the wealth from his precious white gold more than me. This is proof. When I return, I'm going to whip every one of his disobedient slaves because this day of persecution is forever etched in the depths of my heart."

"Silence or I will give the command for you to receive more lashes," said Brigadier General Stevenson.

"You have that so called black Confederate soldier leading the cavalry line with Carter. You are a hypocrite!" exclaimed another deserter who spat on the ground.

"I said silence!" yelled Brigadier General Stevenson, "Don't you boys lose sight of the fact that you have attempted to escape the military duty of our honorable Confederate States Army. Drummers!"

As the drum major counted 39 lashes, the drummers played *The Rogue's March*. Wailing resounded, and fear consumed the onlookers. At the conclusion of the military flogging, the deserters were marched out of Cumberland Gap to the tune of *Yankee Doodle*.

Within the hour, we returned back to camp; and I dismounted Candlelight. Out of nowhere, Jeremiah ran up to me and gave me a big hug. I asked, "Are you okay?"

"Not really. Ah man, did you hear me drumming *Yankee Doodle?* I learned it this morning. This real nice man named Mr. Gunderson spent time with just me; and in no time, I learned every beat. I want to be an enlisted drummer just like Mr. Gunderson when I get older," he said as if he was intentionally changing the subject.

As we walked towards the stables with Candlelight, I said, "I thought you wanted to be a fighting soldier like those black men who are headed to Murfreesborough."

"I still do. I want to go to West Point like Major General Kirby Smith, and then I'll lead thousands of men into battle. I might even be an American President one day," he said pointing proudly to his chest.

"Have you been sipping on Master Green's pot liquor? These bigwigs are never going to let an African become an American President. Did you hear those angry deserters talk about whipping the slaves when they get back home? Miss Celia in Mill Grove was right. We are entangled in freedom."

With bright eyes, Jeremiah said, "Yeah, I heard those deserters, but Master Green has never whipped us. Mr. Gunderson and the other drummers told me to pay them no mind. The drummers say that there are a group of Confederate Generals who are going to ask the Confederate Congress to enlist slaves into regiments for the army."

"Brigadier General Stevenson hasn't even allowed me to face the elephant since we have been here," I said being realistic.

Sounding like a Confederate Major General, Jeremiah said, "You keep up the good work, and you will be the first black General in the army."

"You have been drinking too much of Master Green's pot liquor. By chance, did the drummers give you any names of these Confederate Generals who are proposing to enlist a boat load of slaves in the Confederate States Army?"

Jeremiah stopped walking to gain eye contact with me. With hands extended out from his sides, he proclaimed, "All I know is that Brigadier General Stevenson is talking to some General name Patrick Cleburne about enlisting slaves. I counted at least six General names. Everybody ain't like those deserters, Isaac. You can't give every Confederate a lump of Saint Nic's coal."

"The only thing I have to say to you right now is stop drinking all of that—"

Huffing and puffing, Johnny Reb ran up to me and said, "No need to change. Tie up Candlelight quickly. We have been ordered to help the artillery unit take Long Tom up to the Pinnacle. We are preparing for a battle with Major General

Morgan's Union troops in a few days. The officers received word that the enemy is headed back to Cumberland Gap.

"Are you serious? That cannon weighs tons. It will likely take us days to get Long Tom up the four mile trail to the Pinnacle."

"Not so, Long Tom weighs less than a ton which will make it easy for horses to take it up the mountain," he said swatting a swarm of mosquitoes.

"Horses can handle the transportation of the cannon in the village, but we will need mules to travel up the rocky mountainside. We aren't even with the artillery unit. Why do we have to do all of the hard work anyway?" I asked taking off my Confederate kepi and scratching my head.

Johnny Reb said, "This is our punishment for going to the watering hole last night."

"Are you serious?" I asked putting back on my hat.

"Our punishment is nothing compared to the handful of soldiers from the 3rd Georgia Infantry Battalion," he said pointing.

I was not prepared for what I saw next. A few yards away were Confederate soldiers with fresh open gashes across their backs; and their legs were chained to 12-pound balls. On the way to the artillery unit, we passed the scorned; and their groans were unbearable. I turned to Johnny Reb and said, "If I were you, I'd stay away from that watermelon."

Chapter 16

WHEN I WAS ordered to the picket line south of Cumberland Gap, twelve days had passed since we positioned Long Tom at the Pinnacle. Brigadier General Stevenson ordered an ambush of the Union soldiers who were advancing through the Gap. During an exchange of gunfire, our Confederate forces sustained two casualties with several injured. My job was to escort the hospital's four-wheeled ambulance wagon. After successfully loading up our own, we headed back to Cave Gap at 12:00 in the heat of the day.

Covering us was our Confederate 14th Battalion Tennessee Cavalry. When shots fired through the air, the 14th charged after the approaching enemy. I was caught in the cross-fire as the hospital wagon picked up speed and headed safely towards Cave Gap.

The Confederate cavalry officer waved for me to take cover behind nearby trees and rocks. Shots rang over my head. Therefore, my body remained low as Candlelight sped out of the range of gunfire. When I turned to get a better view, three of our horses with riders fell to the ground. With quickness, the enemy captured our horses, cavalrymen and equipment.

Our Confederate's 14th charged again; however, we were caught in cross-fire by the Union's ambush. A Union private screamed, "We have the rebel flag!"

A Union officer yelled, "5th Tennessee Infantry renew your march to Major General Morgan at Speedwell!"

Then reality hit me. I witnessed history in motion. Our Confederate 14th Battalion Tennessee Cavalry was just in combat with the Union 5th Tennessee Infantry. Neighbor was fighting against neighbor right before my eyes.

When I looked to the ground, a fellow Confederate mounted color guardsman was killed; and the Union private was stripping him of clothing and other articles. When we in the cavalry caused mass confusion, the Union scrambled out of the valley.

I dismounted Candlelight and emerged onto the battlefield. Until his death, the color guardsman could not have lived more than 15 winters. When I turned, Candlelight fled through the density of trees. I lifted the color guardsman and staggered along the trail on foot back to Cave Gap. The rocks were ripping into the soles of my boots. Even though I craved water, every creek was dry because of the June draught. The closer I approached Cave Gap hospital, the more lightheaded I became.

Johnny Reb ran at top speed, gave me aid and carried the color guardsman for the remainder of the way. He said, "The entire Company E was worried sick about your safety."

I could not utter a single word.

When we arrived at Cave Gap, Nurse Minnie felt the forehead of the color guardsman and said, "He's cold as a wagon tire. Put him on that hospital bed." When she gazed into my eyes, she added, "Oh my, you appear dehydrated." Turning to Johnny Reb, she asked, "Do you have any water?"

"Food and water are scarce. The Cumberland River is low. What are we going to do?" Johnny Reb asked in total despair.

She said, "Take this lantern. Follow the trail deep inside the cave until you get to Cleopatra's Pool. There you will find water. Here, fill this jug. Do not tell a soul. This is the reserve we use solely for the sick. Hurry!"

Taking my elbow, Nurse Minnie led me to a bed beside the dead color guardsman.

Then she checked the vital signs of the boy, turned to another nurse, and said, "Go get the doctor. He didn't hang up the fiddle. I feel a pulse."

Within a few minutes, the doctor walked into Cave Gap. Though my vision was blurred, I did see that the color guardsman's limbs were still limp. The doctor said in a Dutch accent, "He has a slight concussion."

Nurse Minnie came over to me and said, "Isaac, right?"

I shook my head.

Holding my hand, she said, "Isaac, you saved this young boy's life. If you would have left him for dead, he would have surely kissed his ancestor's in heaven. God is going to bless you immensely."

The doctor said, "It's a miracle. There is not a mark on his body. The bullet barely grazed the young man's ear. Don't stand there with your mouth full of teeth; pass me that salt of hartshorn." The doctor placed the salt of hartshorn underneath the boy's nose. Within a few minutes, I saw the color guardsman's arm twitch.

"He will come to in no time," Nurse Minnie said smiling at me.

Johnny Reb came from around the corner with the metal jug. As Nurse Minnie passed me the water in a tin cup, she assisted me in sitting up and said, "Steady now."

I cleared my throat and said, "Thank you. Thank you both. All I needed to do was catch my breath. This water from Cleopatra's Pool is the best I've ever tasted. My mother is from Egypt."

Nurse Minnie said, "You don't look Egyptian. You look African."

I said, "I thought Egypt was in Africa."

"Honey, the Egyptians and Asians have been bickering over Egyptian territory for years. Who knows? You might be Asian."

Her remarks were too much for me to comprehend, so I said, "I have to find Candlelight."

The young color guardsman asked, "Where am I?"

The doctor said, "Son, you are at the hospital. Lie back down. You will have to stay here overnight."

He said, "Where are my horse and the battle flag?"

"Ask the cat. You are more important. Just rest," said the doctor.

As we all breathed a sigh of relief, Lieutenant Colonel James Carter walked into Cave Gap and asked, "How are they doing?"

"They will live," said Nurse Minnie.

"We officers have been watching Isaac's military performance. No doubt his living near Emory College has a great deal to do with his advanced communications skills and technical ability. Sergeant Major Green states that Isaac even conducts business for him in the neighboring towns of Oxford, Georgia."

"That doesn't surprise me. The yeoman farmers treat their slaves as an extension of their families." Turning to me, Nurse Minnie said, "Does your master have any children?"

Knowing that I was not to reveal the specifics, I said, "No ma'am. The only children around the farm are me and my brothers."

Nurse Minnie said, "I bet Isaac is like a son to his master. I wonder how he treats Isaac."

Johnny Reb said, "You have already met his master."

Stunned, Nurse Minnie asked, "I have? When?"

"A few days back his master was one of the men who helped Isaac and me bring the injured soldiers to Cave Gap on stretchers," said Johnny Reb.

"Well, I'll be. I don't recall him ordering Isaac around like a slave," she said.

Lieutenant Colonel Carter said, "That's my point. You should meet Isaac's brother Jeremiah who is sharp as a tack. Jeremiah holds perceptive conversations with Brigadier General Stevenson."

"Sounds like a story lifted from the pages of the *King James Bible*," she said assisting me to stand.

"Our officers decided to push the envelope and see how the men would react to Isaac leading the cavalry processional with me. The contention was relatively minimal," said Lieutenant Colonel Carter.

Nurse Minnie said, "I'd say that Isaac here has earned a medal of honor for his bravery today. This young man would have died of starvation or even been killed by wild animals if he were left behind."

Lieutenant Colonel Carter patted me on the back and said, "When you get back to camp, there are a great deal of men from my 14th Battalion Tennessee Cavalry who want to shake your hand. Today you have earned their trust, and that speaks volumes."

Johnny Reb said, "We in the 42nd Regiment Georgia Volunteers Company E believed in Chap Isaac from the start."

"Our cavalrymen say that you were signalling to them from behind the brush with the exact locations of the Union which caused the enemy to scatter across the battlefield," said Lieutenant Colonel Carter looking at me eye to eye.

"I did my best. I really wanted to fight beside them; however, the cavalry officer commanded me to go seek shelter," I said sounding disappointed in myself.

"You did your job as a cavalry scout, and you did that job well."

Master Green walked into Cave Gap and said, "Isaac, I haven't seen you for days. The 14th came back to camp upset that they lost three men but were proud that you helped them save so many more. The entire camp is in a buzz."

"Are the three Confederates now prisoners of war?" I asked wondering if I had been captured what would the Union soldiers have done with me.

"I'm afraid they are. We will do our best to get them back. At the end of the day, your performance was stellar," said Master Green.

"Thank you, sir," I said trying to see myself as he saw me.

Nurse Minnie turned to Master Green and said, "Let me shake your hand; you have raised a fine young man."

For the first time in my life, Master Green was speechless.

Because the hospital area was getting crowded, the temperature began to rise. Sweating profusely, Lieutenant Colonel Carter said to me, "It doesn't take me long to make a decision. Because of your leadership today on the battlefield, I promise that you will be promoted to Corporal in the Confederate States Army."

"That's my boy!" exclaimed Master Green, "I knew he would prove to be one of the best cavalrymen at Cumberland Gap."

"Isaac, we need you to debrief the officers. Come with Sergeant Major Green and me," said Lieutenant Colonel Carter who rubbed his right hand lightly upon the forehead of the young mounted color guardsman.

Nurse Minnie said to the Lieutenant Colonel, "He will be fine. He's in good hands."

As Lieutenant Colonel Carter, Master Green, Johnny Reb and I walked down the hill to camp, Jeremiah was drumming the *Long Roll*. We sprinted towards headquarters. When we entered the log house out of breath, Brigadier General

Stevenson said, "I have orders to move the troops to Tazewell, Tennessee and block Major General Morgan's supply line. We don't have time to break down the tents and pack up equipment. You are to discard everything in sight that belongs to our army, to include the artillery."

I said, "Sir, permission to speak."

"Yes Private, soon to be Corporal," he said winking his eye. "Why would we do that?"

"I am anticipating that after we evacuate, Major General Morgan will place Brigadier General Samuel Carter in command to reoccupy Cumberland Gap. We are not going to leave the Union with a wealth of comfort and vital supplies," said Brigadier General Stevenson.

Taking out his journalist pad and quill, Johnny Reb said, "I can't keep up with all of these Carters. Our Cavalry Colonel James Carter is Confederate. Their Unionist Samuel Carter is a Brigadier General, like our Confederate Brigadier General 'Carter' Stevenson. Did I get that right?"

Lieutenant Colonel James Carter said, "Close enough, therefore, I need you to make sure the men understand the lay of the land. Now, go bury all of the artillery."

I said, "What about Long Tom? It took us a day to get that cannon up to the Pinnacle."

"Pitch it over the side of the mountain," said Brigadier General Stevenson without hesitation.

I asked, "Sir? I don't understand. You want us to roll Long Tom off of the mountain?"

"Private Green, don't ask questions. You have your orders. Move!"

Running towards the Cherokee Artillery unit, I passed along the orders to the artillery officer. I ran to the stables and saddled a gaited mule. Several artillerymen also mounted gaited mules; and we travelled higher and higher to the top of the mountain. I knew we would be at the Pinnacle for a while because the mules were tired and soaked in sweat.

Once we reached Long Tom, we surveyed the terrain below and rolled the cannon to the edge of the cliff. As Long Tom tumbled for yards, one of the wheels came off and rolled down off to the side. I stood at the edge evaluating the value of my role as a cavalry scout. Can critical military operations be sustained without scouts, drummers, teamsters, foragers and cooks?

During our brief break, I decided to take a deep breath of clean air and thank God for allowing me to make it to this mountaintop. The view was simply majestic as the artillerymen pointed out the grand skyline of the Cumberland Mountains and Powell Valley. Their conversations about the bravery of Daniel Boone as a pioneer were uplifting. When I gazed across the horizon, I was the first to see a large body of water which would be vital to our survival during this period of draught.

Chapter 17

MY ACCOLADES FOR pinpointing the locals' water reservoir called Fern Lake were short lived. No sooner did we have water for a few weeks, the entire 2nd Brigade was parched again. I attributed this to the fact that Major General Kirby increased our troop size to 9,000 with several small skirmishes over the summer months.

While Major General Morgan's Union troops were occupying the Pinnacle, Brigadier General Carter Stevenson issued an order to form a perimeter around the outskirts of Cumberland Gap as far as 13 miles out to Tazewell, Tennessee. By September, our Confederated Forces surrounded the Union cutting off their main artery of food, water, and military supplies which also contributed to Morgan's soldiers basically starving to death.

The bigwigs of the Confederate Forces Department of Tennessee were stationed at Castle Rock, a Georgian Plantation owned by Hugh Graham, the founder of Tazewell. On this day, Castle Rock was protected like a fortress by the Confederate States Army. However, the Graham slaves mentioned that the mansion traded hands between the Confederate and Union officers as a headquarters based on who occupied Tazewell at the time.

This was the first time I met all of the slaves who were travelling with the Georgia regimental officers. Josiah, Steve, Henry, Abram and I were in attendance. In no time, I felt as though I slipped back into my native environment on the Green farm, but on a grander scale. Very accustomed to guest, the slaves of Castle Rock opened their slave quarters to us as if we were part of their Master Hugh Graham's Irish royal family.

After I saved the life of the color guardsman, Master Green began to rub elbows with Colonel Henderson, who was on this 6th instant promoting my master from the enlisted rank of Sergeant Major to the officer rank of 2nd Lieutenant in the Confederate States Army. A few hours before dusk, I joined the slaves in setting out several rows of white wooden chairs for the 2nd Brigade military ceremony in the picturesque courtyard.

Walking out of the mansion onto the lawn with Colonel Henderson, Master Green asked, "How do I look in my new uniform?"

"It's such a shame that Mrs. Sally can't fuss over you today," I said sounding like a proud son.

"Did you see all of the books inside the study? I heard that Mr. Graham donates *Bibles* from his collection to the poor. Because he is such a loyal secessionist, I think Mr. Graham has every book except for *Uncle Tom's Cabin.*"

"Don't tell Mr. Graham, a slave of his conducts an evening reading of *Uncle Tom's Cabin* to the entire slave community. Apparently, Tennessee is the only southern state where teaching slaves to read is not punishable by law," I whispered.

Looking back at the 3-story castle, Master Green said, "Thanks for sharing. I was very nervous that the Graham's would find out that Jeremiah and you could read."

"The name fits this place. It does look like a castle positioned on a rock. Mr. Graham is living high on the hog."

Before Master Green could respond, Colonel Henderson said, "The ceremony is about to begin. Will your wife be pinning your new military rank on you today?"

"No, actually I was wondering if it would be out of the question for Isaac or Jeremiah to pin my rank," said Master Green.

A few slaves overheard, and their mouths opened wide.

"I don't mind, let's check with the other officers and Mr. Graham," Colonel Henderson said as he and Master Green headed back into the mansion.

As silence consumed the air, I tried to count the different types of flowers and trees in the garden; however, I lost my place when Josiah said, "I couldn't help but overhear that your master wants you to participate in the ceremony. Don't you fret. My Master Stovall will agree. What's with the long face?"

"My family deserves the lifestyle of Castle Rock. Being here motivates me into working harder to own a track of land in Dublin, Georgia."

Josiah said, "Pray tell, you are at an Irish plantation in Tennessee, and you are headed to be a homeowner in an Irish town in Georgia. Do you know Bill in Dublin?"

"Who is Bill?" I asked surprised that anyone knew a single soul in Dublin.

"Let me see. . . . I think Bill is a servant of the Yopp family. He is serving with his young master in the 14th Georgia Infantry."

"Do say? Is he a fighting soldier?"

"Bill is a drummer like Jeremiah," he said as he searched for Jeremiah in the gathering crowd.

During the ceremony, each slave was to sit with his master. Therefore, we began to walk back towards our seats. I said, "Jeremiah wants to fight like the black confederates who fought in Murfreesborough during the summer. Do you know of any slaves who can vouch that blacks are indeed fighting with Colonel Forrest?"

As we stepped off to the side to wait for our masters, Josiah said, "I sure do. There is a fellow named Louis Napoleon who was recruited to go to war with Colonel Forrest. I think Louis Napoleon is a cook for the Oldham family."

"Have you met him in person?" I asked eager to tell Jeremiah.

"No, I can't say that I have. I just hear folk talk about which slaves are going to have houses and land after the war. Only time will tell how we all fair."

As a group of young ladies passed by, Josiah asked them, "May I help you to your seats?" They giggled. In the distance were Johnny Reb and other young soldiers from the 42nd. However, Mr. Graham gave the girls a disapproving look.

Within a short amount of time, I was seated beside Master Green. I asked, "Did they decide who was going to pin your new military rank?"

"Shhh," said Master Green as Brigadier General Stevenson stood to start the program.

Stevenson spoke about the great sacrifices of our soldiers to include the first Confederate Brigadier General to die in the war, a man named Felix Zollicoffer. Then there was a moment of silence. He continued his speech about hope, charity and love of country. Even though we could hear military shelling with the enemy off into the distance, the mood became festive.

Each man receiving his rank was called to line up in alphabetical order. As Jeremiah and I remained seated, our smiles illuminated the garden.

Within minutes, Brigadier General Stevenson called, "Second Lieutenant Abraham Green."

Master Green walked and stood in line with the other soldiers. To my delight, I was flagged to come up and assist with the pinning. As Master Green smiled, my knees and hands were shaking. Before, I could return to my seat, Brigadier General Stevenson called, "Corporal Isaac Green."

Master Green pulled me by the arm to stand beside him in line. The 42nd soldiers and all of the slaves cheered. In turn,

Master Green pinned my yellow braid design with two adjacent v-shaped strips signifying the corporal rank of cavalry. Though Master Green did not hug me, his tears embraced the essence of my soul. Then Brigadier General Stevenson awarded me the *Medal of Courage*. To be frank, I did not hear another name called. Because there was no way to sketch this event for Rosa Lee, I simply closed my eyes.

After the ceremony, Josiah walked up to me and said, "Congratulations Issac, you are eligible to receive a pension for your service in the Confederate States Army."

"What's a pension?" I asked thinking that my rank and medal was sufficient.

"A pension is money that's awarded to you if you become gravely injured in the war or if your wife becomes a widow."

I chucked and said, "Well, let's not tell my wife, Rosa Lee, about this money."

"Fair enough," he said, "What are you going to do on your furlough?"

"Furlough?"

"Didn't your master tell you? He was granted a furlough to go home as long as he returns as designated for military duty."

"Do Say?" I asked not believing that Master Green would withhold such vital information from me.

Before Josiah could respond, there was an explosion and dirt flew in the air. All of the family, guests, and slaves ran to take cover in the cellar. A few colonels received shelter in a nearby barn. However, Master Green hurried Jeremiah and me into the mansion. He said, "We have to stay together just in case we are needed."

Walking into the kitchen with 12 foot ceilings, Master Green said to Jeremiah, "Go get your drum." Shortly afterwards Brigadier General Stevenson issued the orders. Like clockwork, Jeremiah and I joined Johnny Reb to assume our positions with our Georgia 40th, 42nd, and 52th regiments.

When I turned back to see the splendor of Castle Rock, Mr. Graham was gazing out of his 3rd floor window as if the war were a world stage solely for his observation from the comforts of his Tazewell home. To Mr. Graham the event was already crystal clear. Major General Morgan's Union was attempting to infiltrate our lines near Tazewell. However, this victorious occasion ended with the Union's retreat towards the Cumberland Gap and farther into the back hills of Kentucky. As a cavalry scout, I rushed back to Castle Rock to inform our Confederate Officers.

A great celebration by the Confederacy could be heard throughout the dirt streets of the four square mile rural town. I wish I could say that I faced the elephant and assisted the soldiers in the Battle of Tazewell. Truth be told, having the privilege to pin the rank on Master Green was worth more than the weight of gold. In the morning, we were leaving on a wagon caravan back to Knoxville in order to catch the train back to Atlanta, Georgia.

Master Green was returning to Oxford alive. The question remained: Was he going to be like the Confederate States Army and hold up his end of the bargain?

The Freedom Farm

(October 1862)

Chapter 18

YELLOW, ORANGE, BROWN and burnt red painted the horizon of the Oxford autumn sky on this 15st instance of October. The pebble stone driveway at the Green Farm was a welcomed sight as the wagon pulled up and stopped short of the backyard. Unexpectedly, I heard someone cock a rifle and demand, "Stop! Or I'll kill you."

I said, "Frank is that you? Put that gun down before you hurt somebody."

"Isaac, is that you?" he asked placing the gun by the corner of the house and giving me a big hug. "Where is Master Green?"

"Howdy Frank, I'm glad to see that you protected the farm while I was away," said Master Green.

"Howdy? Where did you learn to speak like that?" he asked looking in the wagon to see if we had any military items.

Master Green said, "I picked up a few words at Cumberland Gap. Where is Sally?"

"She has been missing you something awful. Mrs. Sally and Momma Annabel have gone to Covington to get some cloth."

"My mother has left the farm?" I asked looking around to see if Rosa Lee was nearby.

"After you all left, Momma Annabel and Mrs. Sally have been really close. You don't see one without the other," said Frank grabbing my rebel hat.

"Where is Rosa Lee?"

I didn't like Frank's facial expression when he said, "I think you should ask her yourself."

Master Green said, "What is that suppose to mean? Ask Rosa Lee yourself."

"Come with me," he said putting the grey kepi on his head.

When we turned the corner to the left, everything seemed in place. Master Green breathed a sigh of relief. As we opened up the door to my shotgun slave house, Jacob crawled to the front door. Rosa Lee said, "Frank, I told you to be quiet or you will wake the baby."

Master Green walked inside and asked, "Baby? What baby?"

Jumping to her feet and holding a bundle of joy, Rosa Lee said, "Oh my goodness, you all are back. Frank, hold the baby."

Pushing Master Green to the side, Rosa Lee gave me a big hug while the chocolate Labrador Retriever jumped on my leg.

"Rosa Lee, have you lost your mind?" asked Master Green.

"I'm sorry, Master Green. I was just so excited to see Isaac," she said holding my hand tightly. "This is Ruth. She was born about nine days ago."

Frank said, "You okay, Isaac? I think you should sit down in the rocking chair."

"I have a baby girl?" I asked as Frank gently placed Ruth in my arms, "She is beautiful."

"Frank, are there any more surprises?" asked Master Green.

"I'm afraid to tell you," he said with his head down low.

"What is it?" asked Master Green sternly as he leaned on the doorpost.

"It's Jeremiah. He done run off; and we haven't seen him in months."

Master Green ran out of the door and said, "I almost forgot. We left Jeremiah in the wagon."

While Master Green left to wake up Jeremiah, I said, "Jeremiah met up with us at Camp McDonald and travelled with us to war at Cumberland Gap, Tennessee. He's been with us all of this time."

"You might want to keep Jeremiah away from Momma Annabel when she gets back from town. She says that she is going to kill him if he steps foot back on the farm," said Frank.

Jacob pulled up on my pants leg and toddled across the room. When I laughed, Rosa Lee asked, "What's so funny?"

"My family is beautiful. When did Jacob learn to walk?" I asked passing Rosa Lee the baby and picking up Jacob.

"You haven't said one thing about Cumberland Gap. You have to tell us all about it."

"Maybe tonight during supper . . ." Bouncing Jacob up and down on my knee, he was giggling as if I never left the farm.

Jacob said, "Dada."

I asked, "What did he say?"

Rosa Lee said, "He's been saying 'dada' for weeks. He knows several words, but 'dada' is his favorite."

Jeremiah walked into my house yawning and stretching his arms out wide.

"Boy, what possessed you to run off with the Confederate States Army?" asked Rosa Lee pulling his left ear.

"That hurts," he added, "Where is Momma Annabel?"

"If I were you, I'd go hide underneath the crawlspace. You are in big trouble," she said shaking her index finger.

"Where is Master Green?" I asked.

"He went into the house. He said something about important papers," said Jeremiah.

In a few minutes, Master Green came back into my shotgun house and passed me the deeds to the farmhouse and land in Dublin, Georgia. Then he showed me a legal document which he had drawn up by an attorney in Covington, Georgia. The papers were dated April 12, 1861 and stated that my entire family was free, yet Abraham Lincoln had not yet emancipated the slaves.

Before I could say thank you, Master Green was gone. I hightailed to follow him; however, he locked the backdoor to the main house. As I stood there, Rosa Lee said, "What's wrong?"

I said, "I don't know. He's shut me out."

Coming from around the corner were Mrs. Sally and Momma Annabel carrying bags. Instantly, the packages fell to the ground as Mrs. Sally ran to the backdoor. After banging for a while, Master Green allowed her to enter into the main house.

My entire freed family joined us outside as Momma Annabel hugged me. Then she, likewise, pulled Jeremiah's ear for leaving the farm without permission.

Within a few minutes, Mrs. Sally emerged outside and said, "Isaac, Abraham says that it's best if you all leave."

"Leave? Just like that? Leave?" I asked not understanding what changed so quickly.

Momma Annabel pounded me on my chest and screamed, "I told you not to go off to that war! See what you have done to us, Isaac. We are in exile, just like my father."

"Your father?" I asked holding my mother's hands by her wrists. Then Momma Annabel embraced me and sobbed.

Mrs. Sally said, "Be delighted that you are moving to Dublin and will have a blessed home."

"I want to speak with Master Green now!" I demanded.

"He doesn't know how to tell you the truth," Mrs. Sally said, picking up her hoopskirt to go back into the house. Standing on the top step, she added, "The property in Dublin was your property since your 21st birthday. Your grandsire left it to you."

"My grandsire?"

"Yes, your grandsire. He fought in the Revolutionary War for the United States. Because he fought for America he was exiled from Egypt."

"My grandsire was a black soldier?"

"Yes. Because he could not go back to Egypt to bring his family over to the United States, the Arab-Muslim Slave Trade sold your family in Cairo."

"Are you serious?" I asked still focusing on the fact that I was the second black soldier in my family.

"Your grandsire worked for the Green family in Dublin. They made a deal."

"A deal?"

"If your grandsire voluntarily worked for the Green family until his death, the Green's would buy Annabel and her mother on the slave block in Savannah. Unfortunately, Annabel's mother died on the slave ship. Annabel was reunited as a slave with her father who was already free."

"Let me get this straight. My grandsire was exiled from Egypt because he fought in the Revolutionary War. He made a deal for his family to be sold to the Green family?"

Tears rolled down my mother's eyes and she yelled, "Stop it! Stop it! No more questions."

Mrs. Sally picked up her hoopskirt, came face to face with me, and said, "Your grandsire was a good man. He did what he had to do in order to reunite his family. He served this country well."

Down on her knees my mother pleaded for Mrs. Sally to stop speaking.

"Abraham's father would not disclose the specifics; however, I have always believed your grandsire came from royalty. How else could all of the arrangements been made?" asked Mrs. Sally.

"Royalty?" I asked looking around at my wife and children.

Mrs. Sally continued, "The Dublin house was legally willed to your grandsire by Abraham's father. When your grandsire died, the last will and testament stipulated that the land goes to you, Isaac, upon your 21st birthday."

"I thought we were your slaves, Mrs. Sally."

Momma Annabel pleaded, "Stop it! Stop it!"

"We thought the truth would be too painful for you as a slave," she said extending a loving hand for Momma Annabel to rise. "Your mother is like a sister to me. Your grandsire prayed for the day that all of his family would be free. That day is today."

"So why is Master Green locked up in the main house?" I asked still not understanding after we shared so much over the years.

Placing her left hand on my right shoulder, she said, "Issac, to him, you are a son. Because of generations of hard work, your entire family is finally free."

Mrs. Sally waited for another question; however, I could not cause my mother to suffer long.

With her right hand, Mrs. Sally picked up her hoopskirt again. "Abraham is proud of you, Isaac. We cannot bear to see you go," Mrs. Sally said weeping while her voice cracked. "May God be with you." She gave Momma Annabel a big hug and kiss on the cheek. Hurrying over to Rosa Lee, Mrs. Sally kissed Jacob and Ruth on the forehead. My heart skipped a beat, when the screen door closed.

Jeremiah assisted Momma Annabel in being seated on the top step and said, "Momma Annabel, I'm sorry for running off and planting fear within your heart. I didn't leave you. I went to help Isaac set us free."

Our freed family encircled my mother in love; and I said, "Grandsire sacrificed his entire life. He worked hard so that our family could have our own Green Farm. I wasn't going to allow the War Between the States to rip into the fabric of our grandsire's dreams."

As Momma Annabel wiped the tears from her eyes, Rosa Lee said, "We can stay here and live separately in these four shotgun houses for generations to come. We will be safe and assured to have food." Ruth began to cry, and Rosa Lee rocked her. "Some people will take pleasure in the simplicities of life; and that's fine. However, your Egyptian father possessed bigger dreams for you. He saw you in your own Green Farm."

Jeremiah said, "When I fought in the war—"

We chimed in and said, "Boy, you didn't fight in no war."

With conviction, Jeremiah said, "I did too fight in the war. The soldiers could not move until I tapped the first beat of my drum. I felt powerful. That's how I want you to feel Momma Annabel."

Momma Annabel looked up at her children and said, "The word is empowered. Being given the authority to act and set your own course is good. What you don't realize is that I was raised up with Abraham Green. He is like a brother to me. Some folk spread ugly talk about us, even said that he was abusing me . . . not so. Abraham Green has never laid a hand on me. He is locked up in that house because he don't want us to see him cry. I know him like I know the back of my hand."

As Jeremiah helped her to stand, he said, "We are empowered now to stay here or go to our new home that Grandsire and Isaac fought so hard for. I will tell you this. I saw a big world outside of Oxford with people just like Master Green who were willing to help others."

I said, "We are not exiled from the Green Farm because I fought for the Confederacy. You are feeling the brink of freedom which carries an amount of uncertainty. I can't wait to tell you—" Suddenly, we heard horse hooves and wagon wheels. I changed the subject and said, "I bet that is Mr. Fair coming to see Master Green."

Stepping from around the corner wearing rebel grey were Johnny Reb and two of the soldiers from the 42nd Regiment Georgia Volunteers. Johnny Reb said, "Since we are on furlough, your comrades thought we'd help you move to Dublin. We have three empty wagons. Let's load them up."

Covering her mouth, Momma Annabel cried tears of joy.

Jeremiah ran and gave Johnny Reb a manly hug. As my family and the 42nd soldiers turned to go obtain the little we acquired as slaves, I looked into the main house window. There standing were Master Green and Mrs. Sally, who blew us a kiss.

Entangled in Freedom

Photograph Album
(April 2010)

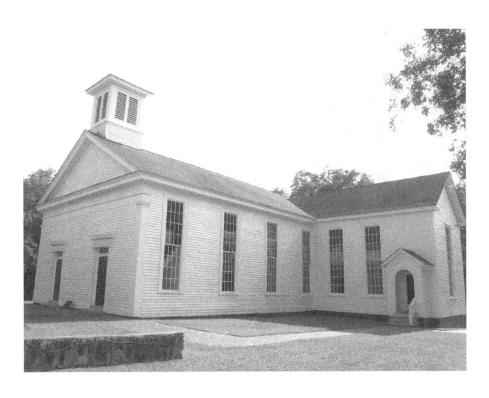

LOCATION: OLD CHURCH (United Methodist Church/ Methodist Episcopal Church South) in Oxford, Georgia.

DESCRIPTION: PICTURED ABOVE is Old Church, where Bishop James O. Andrew ministered. In the 19th century, women were seated on a separate side of the church than men; and slaves sat with their slaveholders. The parishioners, who were not of African descent, led worship on 1st, 2nd, and 3rd Sundays while the slaves were in charge of worship on 4th Sunday at Old Church.

LOCATION: KITTY'S COTTAGE in Oxford, Georgia.

DESCRIPTION: PICTURED ABOVE is the slave home of Kitty, who is historically associated with the splitting of the northern and southern branches of the United Methodist Church due to the complex circumstances of her enslavement.

LOCATION: MABLE HOUSE gravesite in Mableton, Georgia. The town of Mableton is named for Robert Mable and formerly known by many locals as Mill Grove.

DESCRIPTION: PICTURED ABOVE is the headstone of Robert Mable's slaves, who are buried in the same family cemetery with the Mables. In addition, inscribed upon the headstone are the slave names as listed in the 19th century Mable family *Bible.*

LOCATION: MABLE HOUSE in Mableton, Georgia.

DESCRIPTION: PICTURED ABOVE is the rear of the Mable House as viewed by fictitious character Isaac.

LOCATION: GAP CAVE at Cumberland Gap, Tennessee. Gap Cave is also known as Cave Gap, Soldiers' Cave and Cudjo's Cave.

DESCRIPTION: PICTURED ABOVE is the location inside Cave Gap where the Civil War hospital was located.

LOCATION: CUMBERLAND GAP, Tennessee.

DESCRIPTION: PICTURED ABOVE is Cumberland Gap from Pinnacle Outlook in April 2010. Thus, the photo provides a perspective of the views from both the Pinnacle and the valley below as seen 148 years prior (April 1862) by the 42nd Regiment Georgia Volunteers when they arrived at Cumberland Gap. Whether rugged terrain or dense fog, Cumberland Gap was a living element and sometimes a major obstacle to the Union and Confederates as they each skirmished to take control of the Gap. During the War Between the States, Cumberland Gap changed hands several times between the Union and Confederate armies.

Photograph Album Notes:
Kennesaw, Georgia was formerly named Big Shanty, Georgia.
Due to the devastation of the Civil War,
Camp McDonald and the Lacy Hotel no longer exist.

In 1865, the Thirteenth Amendment to the
United States Constitution abolished slavery
as well as involuntary servitude.

On July 26, 1948, President Harry Truman
issued Executive Order 9981 which stated
*"It is hereby declared to be the policy of the President that there shall
be equality of treatment and opportunity for all persons in the armed
services without regard to race, color, religion or national origin."*

Many 20th Century *Bible* commentaries
include clarification that the
"Curse of Ham" has no correlation to
people of African descent.
Also see, Genesis 9:25 *KJV Parallel Bible Commentary*.

Coming From the Rear to Help Advance the Front

◊◊◊◊◊

Forever come from the rear of complacency to the forefront of unparalleled community service in order to unite with others in assuring that our globe remains an informed place to live.
~Ann DeWitt

Entangled in Freedom: A Civil War Story

Ann DeWitt and Kevin M. Weeks

Atlanta, Georgia: August 2010

The Street Life Series Youth Edition—Book 1

Places of Literary Refuge in Dublin, Georgia:
LaQuinta Inns and Suites
Longhorn Steakhouse
Page House Bed & Breakfast

Beverage Enjoyed during Brainstorming Sessions
Cumberland Gap Spring Water
Middlesboro Coca-Cola Bottling Works, Inc. (MCCBW)

SOURCES

The following citations were used as sources of information in writing this novel.

2nd South Carolina String Band. "Cumberland Gap." *Online Posting.* YouTube, 21 June 2008. Web. 1 May 2010.

A Man with a Message by Nelson Winbush. DVD. Dixie Depot, 2008.

"A Rebel Captain Forcing Negroes To Load Cannon." New York: Harper's Weekly. 10 May 1862, VOL. VI ed., No. 280. sec. Print.

"African-American Postal Workers in the 19th Century." United States Postal Service. Web. 1 May 2010. <http://www.usps.com/postalhistory/_pdf/AfricanAmericanWorkers19thc.pdf>

"American Civil War Battle Statistic: Commanders and Casualties." americancivilwar.com. Web. 1 May 2010. <http://americancivilwar.com/cwstats.html>

Auslander, Mark. "The Myth of Kitty: Paradoxes of Blood, Law and Slavery in a Georgia Community." Georgia: Oxford College of Emory University. Web. 1 May 2010. <http://www.marial.emory.edu/pdfs/kittydoc.pdf>

Barrow, Charles Kelly., and J. H. Segars. *Black Southerners in Confederate Armies: a Collection of Historical Accounts.* Gretna, LA: Pelican, 2007. Print.

—.*Forgotten Confederates: An Anthology About Black Southerners.* Atlanta, GA: Southern Heritage Press, 1995. Print.

Battles and Leaders of the Civil War: Volume Three. New-York: The Century Company, 1884. Print.

Black Confederates by Dr. Edward C. Smith. DVD. Dixie Rising, 2008.

"Black History Month: Black Confederate Heritage." Sons of Confederate Veterans Education Committee. Web. 1 May 2010. <http://www.scv.org/documents/edpapers/blackhistory.pdf>

Bonds, Russell S. *Stealing the General.* Pennsylvania: Westholme Publishing, LLC, 2007. Print.

"Bruce & Emmet's Drummers and Fifers Guide." Fife & Drum Online. Web. 1 May 2010. <http://www.fifedrum.org/resources/music/be/>

"Bugle Calls." Military Analysis Network. Web. 1 May 2010. <http://www.fas.org/man/dod-101/sys/land/bugle.htm>

Calhoun, Captain W. L. *History of the 42nd Regiment Georgia Volunteers, Confederate States Army.* Atlanta, Georgia, 1900. Print.

"Carter's Tennessee Cavalry Regiment." TNGenWeb Project, 1964. Web. 1 May 2010. <http://www.tngenweb.org/civilwar/csacav/csa1carte>

"Civil War." History.com. Web. 1 May 2010. <http://www. history.com/this-day-in-history/11/11?catId=2>

"Civil War Horses." Suite101.com, 14 November 2007. Web. 1 May 2010. <http://us-civil-war.suite101.com/article.cfm/ the_gettysburg_horse_sacrifice>

"Civil War Memory: Patrick Cleburne and Black Confederates Take Hollywood." 2 February 2010. Web. 1 May 2010. <http://cwmemory.com/2010/02/05/patrick-cleburne-and-black-confederates-take-hollywood>

"Civil War Re-enactment at Cumberland Gap." 10 vols. *Online Posting.* YouTube, 21 July 2009. Web. 1 May 2010.

Clarke, H.C. *Confederate States Almanac and Repository of Useful Knowledge for 1862.* Mississippi. Print.

Cleburne, Pat. "Negroes In our Army." civilwarhome.com. 5 August 1904. Web. 1 May 2010. <http://www.civilwarhome. com/negrosinarmy.htm>

"Confederate Flag." The Civil War. Web. 1 May 2010. <http:// www.sonofthesouth.net/leefoundation/Confederate_Flag. htm>

"Confederate Flag History." Web. 1 May 2010. <http://www. scv674.org/csaflags.htm>

"Controversies & Enigmas: The Bishop, His Slave and the Church." Emory History. Web. 1 May 2010. <http:// emoryhistory.emory.edu/enigmas/Kitty.htm>

Cox, Jack F. *The 1850 Census of Georgia Slave Owners.* Baltimore, Maryland: Clearfield, 1999. Print.

"Cumberland Gap." Web. 1 May 2010. <http://www.traditionalmusic.co.uk/folk-song-lyrics/Cumberland_Gap.htm>

"Cumberland Gap." Public.Resource.Org, 1986. YouTube. Web. 1 May 2010.

Daniel, Larry J. *Soldiering in the Army of Tennessee: A Portrait of Life in a Confederate Army.* University of North Carolina Press, 1991: 32. Print.

Davis, Althea T. *Early Black American Leaders in Nursing: Architects for Integration and Equality.* London: Jones and Bartlett Publishers, Inc and National League for Nursing, 1999: 19. Print.

DeWitt, Ann. *Black Confederate Soldiers.* Web. 1 May 2010. <http://www.blackconfederatesoldiers.com>

Echoes of Glory: Arms and Equipment of the Confederacy. Virginia: Time Life Books, 1996: 251. Print.

"Emory History." Unigo.com. Web. 1 May 2010. <http://www.unigo.com/emory_university/information>

"Executive Order 9981." Harry S. Truman Library & Museum. Web. 1 May 2010. <http://www.trumanlibrary.org/9981a.htm>

"For Us or Against Us." New York: Harper's Weekly. 10 May 1862: 291, VOL. VI ed., No. 280. sec. Print.

"General Barton & Stovall History ~ Heritage Association." GBSHHA. Web. 1 May 2010. <http://www.generalbartonandstovall.com>

"General G.W. Morgan's Report: Letter from the Secretary of War." House of Representatives, Ex. Doc. No. 94. 27 May 1864. Print.

"Genesis 9.18-26." *Bible: King James Version.* BibleGateway.com. Web. 1 May 2010.

Goodson, Gary Ray. *Georgia Confederate 7,000.* 3 vols. Shawnee, Colorado: Goodson Enterprises, Inc., 2000 Print.

Hadley, Craig. "A 19th Century Slang Dictionary." Web. 1 May 2010. <http://www.rugglesrag.com>

Hamilton, West A. "The Negroes' Historical and Contemporary Role in National Defense: Hampton Conference on National Defense." November 26, 1940." Harry S. Truman Library & Museum. Web. 1 May 2010. <http://www.trumanlibrary.org>

"Henry William Paris." McHugh/Paris Genealogy. Web. 1 May 2010. <http://donmchugh.tripod.com/paris/hwparis.htm#Henry%20William%20Paris>

Herzog, Johann, Philip Schaff and Albert Hauk. *The New Schaff-Herzog Encyclopedia of Religious Knowledge.* New York: Funk and Wagnalls Company, 1914: 349. Print.

"History of the Christian Methodist Episcopal Church." Web. 1 May 2010. <http://www.godonthe.net/cme/history/cme_hist.htm>

"House Types in Georgia." Historic Preservation Division. Georgia. Web. 1 May 2010. < http://gashpo.org/assets/documents/housetypes.pdf>

Howell, Elmo. *Mississippi Back Roads: Notes on Literature and History*. Memphis, Tenn.: Langford & Associates, 1998. Print.

Inscoe, John C. *Appalachians and Race: The Mountain South from Slavery to Segregation*. Lexington, Kentucky: The University Press of Kentucky, 2001. Print.

"Jefferson Davis." Jeffersondavis.net. Web. 1 May 2010. <http://www.jeffersondavis.net/>

Kincaid, Robert. *The Wilderness Road*. Tennessee: Lincoln Memorial University, 1990: 238-246. Print.

"Kitty's Cottage and the Methodist Civil War." Georgia: Emory University, 2007. Web. 1 May 2010. <http://www.emory.edu/EMORY_MAGAZINE/fall97/enigma.html>

"Larned, Johney. *Though Silent, They Speak*. Illinois: Xlibris Corporation, 2006: 107. Print.

Lesher, James H. *Xenophanes of Colophon: Fragments: A Text and Translation with a Commentary*. Canada: University of Toronto Press Incorporated, 1992: 197. Print.

Luckett, William W. *Cumberland Gap National Historical Park*. Tennessee: The Tennessee Historical Society, 1964. Vol. XXIII, No. 4 Print.

"Nursing in the Civil War South." Civilwarwomenblog.com. 17 Nov. 2006. Web. 1 May 2010. <http://www.civilwarwomenblog.com/2006/11/nursing-in-civil-war-south.html>

Matthews, James Muscoe. *Public Laws of the Confederate States of America: Passed at the First Session of the First Congress.* Richmond: R. M. Smith, Printer to Congress, 1862: 29. Print.

Miller, Edward A. "Garland H. White, black army chaplain." HighBeam Research. 1997 September 1. Web. 1 May 2010. <http://www.highbeam.com/doc/1G1-20378612.html>

"Monroe signs the Missouri Compromise." History Channel. 6 March 1820. Web. 1 May 2010. <http://www.history.com/this-day-in-history/monroe-signs-the-missouri-compromise>

Murphy, R.C. "The Civil War Drummer." Wild Cat Band. Web. 1 May 2010. <http://www.wildcatband.com/ropedrums.html>

Powell, Marilyn. *Cool: The Story of Ice Cream.* Toronto, Ontario: Penguin Books Canada, 2005. Print.

"Psalms 20.7." *Bible: King James Version.* BibleGateway.com. Web. 1 May 2010.

"Psalms 22.6." *Bible: King James Version.* BibleGateway.com. Web. 1 May 2010.

"Psalms 121.1." *Bible: King James Version.* BibleGateway.com. Web. 1 May 2010.

"Ranks and Insignia of the Confederate States." Wikipedia. Web. 1 May 2010. <http://en.wikipedia.org/wiki/Ranks_and_insignia_of_the_Confederate_States>

Robinson, Willie L. "Tennessee Colored Pension Applications for CSA: Tennessee Colored Pension Application for CSA Service." Web. 1 May 2010. <http://users.ameritech.net/michael648/CwVetsFrame.html>

Russell, Lawrence T. *Civil War: Arms & Firepower.* Gettysburg, PA. Print.

Seabrook, Lochlainn. *National Bedford Forrest: Southern Hero, American Patriot.* Franklin, Tennessee: Sea Raven Press, 2010. Print.

Shavin, Norman. *The Atlanta Century.* Atlanta, Georgia: Capricorn Corporation, 1865. Print.

Shellnutt, James. "The 42nd Georgia Historical Document." Web. 1 May 2010. <http://www.42ndgeorgia.com>

"Slavery." The Tennessee Encyclopedia of History and Culture. Web. 1 May 2010. <http://tennesseeencyclopedia.net>

Smiley, Tavis. "The Curse of Ham: Slavery and the Old Testament." NPR, 15 December 2003. Web. 1 May 2010. <http://www.npr.org/templates/dmg/dmg.php?prgCode=TAVIS&showDate=15-Dec-2003&segNum=2&NPRMediaPref=WM>

"Soldier." Def. 2. *Merriam-Webster Online.* Merriam-Webster, 2010. Web. 1 May 2010. <http://www.webster.com>

Stager, Claudette and Martha Carver. *Looking Beyond the Highway: Dixie Road and Culture.* Tennessee: The University of Tennessee Press/Knoxville. 2006: 168-181. Print.

"The Civil War." Son of the South, 2003. Web. 1 May. 2010. <http://www.sonofthesouth.net/>.

"The Civil War in Georgia: Georgia 42nd Infantry Regiment." Web. 1 May 2010. <http://www.researchonline.net>

The Great Locomotive Chase (1956). Lawrence Edward Watkin and Walt Disney, Producers. Francis D. Lyon, Dir. Fress Parker and Jeffrey Hunter, Actors. DVD. Walt Disney Video, 2004.

"The Story of 'Jack' Daniel." Tennessee History Classroom: Full History Stories. Web. 1 May 2010. <http://www.tennesseehistory.com/class/JD.htm>

"Thomas R.R. Cobb (1823-1862)." The New Georgia Encyclopedia. Web. 1 May 2010. <http://www.georgiaencyclopedia.org/nge/Article.jsp?id=h-2487>

Trowbridge, J.T. *Cudjo's Cave.* Boston: Lee and Shepard Publishers, 1904. Print.

"U.S. Civil War History & Genealogy." Genealogyforum.com. Web. 1 May 2010. <http://www.genealogyforum.com/gfaol/resource/Military/Drummer.htm>

"U.S. Constitution: Thirteenth Amendment." FindLaw for Legal Professionals. Web. 1 May 2010. <http://caselaw.lp.findlaw.com/data/constitution/amendment13>

Vaughan, David Wynn. "A Brief History of the Georgia Military Institute and a Study of Its Uniform 1851-1864." BNET, 2004. Web. 1 May 2010. <http://findarticles.com/p/articles/mi_qa3905/is_200409/ai_n9457063>

Walker, Annie Kendrick. *Memoirs of the Graham Family*. New York: Tobias A. Wright, Publisher, 1876. Print.

Watson, Paul. "Confederate Forces—Department of East Tennessee: May 31st—December 27th 1862." 29 March 2005. Web. 1 May 2010. <http://orbat.com/site/history/volume4/435/Department%20of%20East%20Tennessee%20 1862.htm>

Weeks, Kevin M. *The Street Life Series: Is it Rags or Riches?* Philadelphia, Pennsylvania: Xlibris Corporation, 2009. Print.

Welsh, Jack D. *Medical Histories of Confederate Generals*. Ohio: Kent State University Press, 1995: 207. Print.

Williams, Richard G. *Stonewall Jackson: The Black Man's Friend*. Tennessee: Cumberland House Publishing, Inc. 2006. Print.

CPSIA information can be obtained
at www.ICGtesting.com
Printed in the USA
LVHW090107010421
683128LV00016B/178/J